PUFFIN BOOKS

The Silver Dolphin

Born in Hertfordshire, England, on 29 May 1952, Louise Cooper describes herself as 'a typical scatter-brained Gemini'. She spent most of her school years writing stories when she should have been concentrating on lessons, and her first fantasy novel, *The Book of Paradox*, was published in 1973, when she was just twenty years old. Since then she has published more than sixty books for adults and children.

Louise now lives in Cornwall with her husband, Cas Sandall. When she isn't writing, she enjoys singing (and playing various instruments), cooking, gardening, 'messing about on the beach' and – just to make sure she keeps busy – is also treasurer of her local Royal National Lifeboat Institution branch.

Visit Louise at her own website at louisecooper.com

Books by Louise Cooper

Sea Horses series in reading order

Sea Horses
The Talisman
Gathering Storm
The Last Secret

Mermaid Curse series in reading order

The Silver Dolphin
The Black Pearl

mermaid curse

The Silver Dolphin

LOUISE COOPER

PUFFIN

PUFFIN BOOKS

Published by the Penguin Group
Penguin Books Ltd, 80 Strand, London WC2R ORL, England
Penguin Group (USA) Inc., 375 Hudson Street, New York, New York 10014, USA
Penguin Group (Canada), 90 Eglinton Avenue East, Suite 700, Toronto, Ontario, Canada M4P 2Y3
(a division of Pearson Penguin Canada Inc.)
Penguin Ireland, 25 St Stephen's Green, Dublin 2, Ireland (a division of Penguin Books Ltd)
Penguin Group (Australia), 250 Camberwell Road, Camberwell, Victoria 3124, Australia
(a division of Pearson Australia Group Pty Ltd)
Penguin Books India Pvt Ltd, 11 Community Centre, Panchsheel Park,
New Delhi – 110 017, India
Penguin Group (NZ), 67 Apollo Drive, Rosedale, North Shore 0632, New Zealand
(a division of Pearson New Zealand Ltd)
Penguin Books (South Africa) (Pty) Ltd, 24 Sturdee Avenue, Rosebank, Johannesburg 2196,
South Africa

Penguin Books Ltd, Registered Offices: 80 Strand, London WC2R ORL, England

puffinbooks.com

First published 2008
3

Text copyright © Louise Cooper, 2008
All rights reserved

The moral right of the author and illustrator has been asserted

Set in Sabon by Palimpsest Book Production Limited,
Grangemouth, Stirlingshire
Made and printed in England by Clays Ltd, St Ives plc

British Library Cataloguing in Publication Data
A CIP catalogue record for this book is available from the British Library

ISBN: 978-0-141-32225-4

www.greenpenguin.co.uk

Mixed Sources
Product group from well-managed
forests and other controlled sources
www.fsc.org Cert no. SA-COC-1592
© 1996 Forest Stewardship Council

*For my lovely mother, Pat,
with eternal thanks for bringing me
to Cornwall at a very early age
and introducing me to the land that
is truly home*

Prologue

Light shimmered in the undersea cave, sending dancing reflections across the walls and over the surface of the huge calm pool in the centre. On the walls of the cave were nine mirrors that looked as though they were made of rippling water. Each mirror glowed a different colour. Seven were the hues of the rainbow: red, orange, yellow, green, blue, indigo and violet; the other two shone silver and black. Vague, graceful images moved and drifted in the depths of the rainbow-coloured mirrors. The black and the silver, though, showed no reflections at all, but were still and quiet.

At one side of the cave was a couch of rock, draped with many-coloured seaweeds like luxurious cushions, and decorated with shells and mother-of-pearl and all manner of sea trinkets. On the couch sat a mermaid. She had blue-black hair that fell in a shining curtain to her waist, and eyes as green and brilliant as emeralds. Around her shoulders she wore a regal cloak of woven seaweed, and there were rings on her fingers and more sea-jewels at her wrists and throat. She was as beautiful as the cave, but there was a cruel edge to her lovely face as she stared at a circlet that she held in her hands. The circlet was made of gold, and round its edge, evenly spaced, pearls were set. Each pearl was a different colour. There were settings for nine – but two were missing.

The mermaid's eyes were as cold as frost. 'Only seven,' she muttered. 'Only *seven*.

I must have *all* the pearls, or my power will not be complete!' Her expression twisted angrily. 'It was the dolphins who thwarted me – Arhans and her interfering friends – I will have revenge on them, I swear it!'

The creature coiled at the foot of the rock stirred and raised its dark, ugly head. 'Majesty, that will not be easy,' it said. 'The dolphins consider themselves beyond anyone's command – even that of such a great Queen as you.'

'Oh, I know, Tullor. But, even if I cannot hurt them, I can do whatever I please to anyone who sides with them. Someone must know who has the two missing pearls. And they will tell us.'

The creature's mouth opened, revealing rows of ferocious teeth, and it hissed with pleasure. 'We will *make* them tell, Majesty!'

'That's right, my faithful servant. The old Queen is dead, and her daughter is . . . shall we say . . . *lost*.' She smiled cruelly. '*I* am

Queen now. I will find the missing pearls.
And when I have them, and the crown of
power is whole again, no one will be able to
defy me. They will not dare – and I will rule
forever!'

Chapter One

'This,' said Lizzy Baxter breathlessly, tossing her unruly blonde hair out of her eyes, 'is *hopeless*!'

Her elder sister, Rose, gave her own end of the cardboard box another tug, but only succeeded in wedging it more tightly in the bend of the stairs. Then the box slipped and fell on Lizzy's toe, and she said a rude word.

'Better get Dad to help,' Rose puffed. 'Honestly, I can't see why on *earth* we had to move to a house where everything's too narrow or too twisty or both! Why couldn't we have found somewhere modern?'

Ignoring the grumbles, Lizzy looked over her shoulder, down to the cluttered hall, and yelled, 'DA-ad! We can't shift it!'

Mr Baxter appeared, tousled and with smears of dust all over his shirt. 'I told you to leave it to Mum and me,' he said, pounding up the stairs. His feet clattered like horses' hooves on the bare wood. 'Out of the way, Lizzy; that's it . . . Now, Rose, if you just get a good grip on your end and pull . . .'

Moving house, Lizzy decided later, had to be the craziest and most exhausting experience in the whole world. But it was also just about the best fun she had ever had. Take this evening, for instance. All the furniture was finally in the right rooms, and they had eventually found enough duvets and pillows to make up the beds. But the electricity hadn't been reconnected yet, so now all four Baxters were sitting by candlelight in a kitchen full of crates and boxes, eating baked beans and sausages cooked on a camping stove, with lemonade and cider to wash it down. It had to be the wackiest picnic ever.

'Well, I don't care what you say, Rose,' Mrs Baxter mumbled through a mouthful of food, '*I* think it's a fabulous house! What about you, Lizzy, love?'

Lizzy stared at the dark square of the window (the curtains weren't up yet). She couldn't see the small garden now, or the other houses beyond, scrambling further up the steep hill of this Cornish fishing port. But a warm feeling was growing in her that had nothing to do with the food.

'I love it,' she said firmly. 'It feels like home.'

Lizzy was too excited to sleep. At midnight she was still sitting at the window of her new bedroom, from where she could see the harbour. The house had thick stone walls, and the window was set into a deep alcove that made a perfect lookout seat.

Everything was very quiet. There was no traffic noise, and now that the rain had stopped the only sound she could hear was the sighing murmur of the sea. Every few seconds, the beam of a lighthouse swung round and round, turning constantly over the water in its unending warning circle. The lighthouse was a small automatic one that stood on the jutting headland between the beach and the harbour. Tomorrow, Lizzy thought, she would see it for herself. And that thought set her wondering about what she had said earlier.

It feels like home. And maybe it was . . .

Lizzy and Rose had known for a long time that the people they called Mum and Dad were not their real parents. Mr and Mrs Baxter couldn't have children of their own. They had adopted Rose when she was one, and a few years later they had adopted baby Lizzy too. As soon as the girls were old enough they had told them the truth. Rose's parents had been killed in a car crash. The Baxters knew their names and where they had come from. But with Lizzy, it was different. She had been found abandoned when she was only a few months old. No family could be traced, so she was taken into a children's home and put up for adoption soon afterwards. And, strangely, the place where she had been found was not far from this town.

It was a coincidence, of course, that she had come to live in the area again. Dad taught English Literature at university, and when he had been offered a post at the new university in Cornwall, all the family had jumped at the chance to live by the sea. Dad and Mum had asked Lizzy if she minded coming here, which she thought was very considerate of them. But it didn't make her feel uncomfortable. Quite the opposite, in fact; she had *wanted* to come.

The lighthouse beam swung round again,

gleaming on the sea's surface and turning it briefly from midnight black to shimmering silver-grey. Lizzy blinked as a funny little tingling sensation moved in her stomach. The quiet harbour, the ever-turning light . . . Might she have seen them before? She would have been too young to remember, but could it be the reason why she just *knew* she was going to be happy here?

She put a hand to her throat, and her fingers closed round something that hung there on a silver chain. It was a locket, made from mother-of-pearl that shone with rainbow colours. It had been round Lizzy's neck when she was found, but no one knew who had given it to her.

Lizzy pressed a tiny catch and the locket opened like the two halves of a shell. Inside was a single curl of hair, the same bright, pale blonde as her own. It was a very unusual colour, and everyone else believed it must be Lizzy's. But Lizzy secretly believed the curl of hair belonged to her mother or father, and in her mind it was the one link she had with the parents she had never known.

There were footsteps on the landing outside, then her door opened and Mum looked in.

'Hey, you should be asleep!' she said, smiling.

Lizzy smiled back, closing the locket and letting it fall back on its chain. 'Sorry, Mum. I was too excited.'

'I know, love. It's always strange, the first night in a new house. But we've got lots to do tomorrow, so get into bed now, all right?'

Mum understood. Lizzy nodded. 'All right,' she said.

'Night, night.' Mum came across and kissed her. 'Sleep tight.'

Lizzy grinned. 'Don't let the bedbugs bite!'

They both laughed at the old rhyme, and Mum went out again, closing the door softly.

Lizzy waited until the lighthouse beam had flashed round once more. Then she slipped under her duvet, snuggled down and closed her eyes.

Within two days the whirl of unpacking and putting things away was over. The house was 'coming along', as Mum put it; the electricity and phone had been connected, and even Dad's tiny downstairs study didn't look like the result of a whirlwind in a paper factory. So Lizzy and Rose were allowed time off to start exploring their new surroundings in earnest.

At first they went out together, getting to know the layout of the town and which streets led where. But although the two girls were good friends, Rose at fifteen was four years older than Lizzy, and what she really wanted was to make new friends. Especially boys. Lizzy wasn't exactly a nuisance, but Rose had her own kind of exploring to do.

So it wasn't long before Lizzy found herself on her own.

She didn't mind at all. The town was fascinating, and she could happily have spent weeks just wandering around. In fact there was *so* much to see and to discover that she hardly knew where to start. This wasn't a small sleepy village like the Cornwall she had always imagined, but a working fishing port, busy and bustling and filled with activity. With summer in full swing it was crowded with holiday visitors too, and everyone looked healthy and happy and smiled at each other. It was, Lizzy thought, like a huge and lively fairground.

The harbour was a short walk from the Baxters' house, down through narrow streets to the foot of the hill. It wasn't a picture-postcard harbour: instead of sailing boats there were fishing trawlers crowded at the old stone quay, a big warehouse and covered fish market with forklift trucks running backwards and forwards, wind-tanned men in overalls and heavy boots. The mixed smells of brine, fish and diesel fuel made Lizzy's nose wrinkle, and everywhere there were gulls, flapping and diving and shrieking.

Beyond the quay and the warehouse were more boats, smaller ones, moored at a network of floating wooden jetties, which Lizzy learned were called pontoons. The port's lifeboat station was nearby, with the splendid orange and blue lifeboat rocking at its own special pontoon. And when you looked out past the crowded harbour, there was the great sweep of the bay, with the ancient castle of St Michael's Mount standing up tall and magnificent from the surrounding sea.

The whole bay was fringed with golden beaches, and the town's own beach was separated from the harbour by the lighthouse headland. It was a wonderful place, with fine, white sand that seemed to stretch away for miles. Lizzy walked the length of it among the holiday crowds, exploring rock pools and jumping over the incoming waves as they played themselves out in the shallows. There was a safe bathing area patrolled by lifeguards. Lizzy was a good swimmer; at her last school she had been by far the best in her year. The sea was much colder than a swimming pool, but Mum and Dad had bought her a wetsuit as a 'moving in' present, and she was delighted to have the chance to use it.

Lizzy was swimming in her new suit, rolling over in the waves and pretending to be a seal, when shouts from the shore caught her attention. As she stood up she saw people pointing out to sea. About fifty metres offshore were five dolphins. They were streaking across the bay, and then suddenly, as one, they leaped clear of the water, twisting gracefully in mid-air and plunging down again with barely a splash. Lizzy watched in delight and admiration, and had a sudden wild wish to swim to where they were and play with them, like a dolphin herself.

A voice nearby said, 'Fantastic, aren't they?' and Lizzy turned to see one of the lifeguards, a fair-haired Australian whom she had talked to once or twice, grinning at her.

'They're amazing!' she agreed eagerly.

'We often see them around here,' the lifeguard told her. 'They don't usually come this close to shore, though. Must have seen something that interests them.'

For no reason at all a funny little shiver went through Lizzy as he said that. 'I'd love to get closer to them,' she said.

'Yeah? You ought to go out on a Sea Safari trip, then. A guy called Dave Pengelly runs them from the harbour. He takes people right along the coast specially to watch dolphins. There are other creatures too – you'll see basking sharks, and the caves where the seals live.'

Lizzy's eyes lit up. 'That would be so cool!'

'Ask your mum and dad, then. They'll probably want to go as well. It's worth seeing.' The lifeguard smiled again. 'I'd better get back to work. Take care in the sea, yeah? Don't go out of your depth.'

He strolled away along the beach. The dolphins were still visible, but they were moving further away. Lizzy stared after them until the bright sun hurt her eyes. Then she walked back to where she had left her towel, and flopped down on the sand. She would ask Mum and Dad about the Sea Safari as soon as she got home.

Chapter Two

Rose thought the Sea Safari was a brilliant idea, and to the girls' delight Mr and Mrs Baxter didn't take much persuading. The next day was fine, with a mixture of sunshine and cloud, so as soon as lunch was finished they all headed for the harbour and booked on the next two-hour trip.

The boat was called the *Sea Lion*, and it was the strangest boat Lizzy had ever seen. The twelve seats inside the inflatable rubber hull looked like motorbike saddles arranged in pairs. The passengers sat astride and hung on to grab-handles, while Dave Pengelly –

who was very young and good-looking, much to Rose's approval – stood at the controls behind them.

Dad was eager to show off his knowledge. 'This kind of boat's known as a RIB,' he told the girls.

'Rib?' said Rose. 'That's a silly name! It doesn't look anything like someone's rib!'

Dad laughed. 'It stands for Rigid Inflatable Boat. They're very stable – and very fast.'

They found out how fast when they swung out from the harbour and headed towards the open sea. The Mount with its castle passed by on the left side ('Port side', Dad corrected smugly when Rose got it wrong), then the engine roared into full life. The ride was exhilarating. The boat skimmed over the water as though it were on skis, and every time they hit a swell, or the wash from another boat, they seemed to take off and fly, coming down again with a jolt that sent a burst of spray glittering into the air. The wind whipped Lizzy's hair and blew salty-tasting strands into her mouth. She pretended she was riding a dolphin, and that the excited shrieks of the two middle-aged women in front of her were the dolphins' cries as they forged through the water.

'You two enjoying it?' Dad shouted over the noise of the engine.

'It's *fantastic*!' Lizzy called back. Rose was looking a bit green, but she nodded determinedly. 'Yeah – great, Dad . . .'

Soon, though, the wild ride was over and the boat slowed down to a gentler speed as they left the bay behind and moved down the coast, following a line of high, craggy cliffs. Rocks jutted up from the water at the cliffs' feet, and beyond the rocks were caves like dark, gaping mouths. Switching on a microphone, Dave Pengelly began to give a commentary. This was where the seals lived and bred, he told them. All the caves had names – there was Cat and Mouse, Echo

Cave and the big one – 'just up ahead, where the waves are breaking' – was called the Deadman. Looking at the tide slapping dark and dangerous at the entrance, Lizzy could imagine how it got its name, and shivered.

Everyone was looking for a glimpse of the seals as they passed the caves, but there were none to be seen. Nor were there any dolphins either, which was very disappointing. It was just one of those things, said Dave. Sometimes they appeared, sometimes they didn't, and you couldn't predict. Rose, who was feeling better now that they were moving more slowly, grinned at Lizzy and said, 'Maybe they ought to get some tame ones, and train them to come when they're called.'

Lizzy smiled back but said nothing. The ride was wonderful anyway; just the feeling of being out here, with nothing but shining sea in every direction, was more than enough.

After a while they gave up the search and turned back towards the harbour. The boat speeded up again, and was powering over the water when someone pointed further out to sea and shouted, 'Look – oh, look!'

It was the dolphins. They came streaking towards the boat, sunlight glinting on their backs. They were moving so fast that Lizzy thought they must surely crash into the side of the *Sea Lion*. But at the last moment they swerved, then suddenly, incredibly, they were playing alongside, just metres from the astonished passengers. One leaped right out of the water, twisting in mid-air. Lizzy just had time to glimpse a silvery streak along its back before it plunged down again and dived under the boat, to emerge on the other side. Cries of delight went up, and even Dave Pengelly was staring in amazement.

'This is something special!' he called over the microphone. 'I've never known them do that before. You don't know how lucky we are!'

The dolphin with the silver streak was on Lizzy's side of the boat now. She leaned over, her eyes shining, and it seemed to her that the dolphin looked back at her. Its eyes weren't like a fish's eyes at all, but warm and intelligent as any human's. *But of course dolphins aren't fish*, she reminded herself. *They're mammals, just like us.*

As if it had heard and understood, the dolphin made a chittering noise that sounded very much like laughter. Lizzy laughed too. It seemed that this particular dolphin wanted to be friends. In fact she could almost believe that it had come to see her and no one else. What had she said to the lifeguard yesterday? '*I'd love to get closer to them.*' Well, her wish really had come true.

The other dolphins dropped back as the boat headed towards land, but the silver-streaked dolphin – *her* dolphin, Lizzy thought, though she knew the idea was foolish – kept pace with them. It was so close that she could almost have reached out and touched it. Suddenly she couldn't resist the temptation, and she *did* reach out, stretching one hand towards the beautiful creature.

'Lizzy!' Mum called anxiously from behind her. 'Don't be so silly – sit up!' She grasped Lizzy's shoulder, pulling her back. As Lizzy straightened, she felt something tangle in the straps of the lifejacket she was wearing. There was a faint snapping noise, and a small object dropped from her neck and bounced on to the boat's side.

'My locket!' Lizzy's delight turned to dismay. She made a wild grab, but before she could reach it, the locket slid off the smooth, slippery rubber hull, fell into the sea – and vanished.

'No, oh, no!' Lizzy cried. 'It's gone! My locket's gone!'

For a moment she had an overwhelming urge to dive into the sea and try to get the locket back before it sank out of reach. But the moment passed. The locket was already gone, and there was nothing she could do. There was nothing anyone could do.

The dolphins had turned back out to sea but Lizzy didn't watch them as they sped away. All she could think about was her locket. It had been her only link with her real parents, and now it was lost forever. The family all tried to console her, but she was too heartbroken to be comforted. Besides, what could they say? No words could make any difference.

The boat chugged on while Lizzy sat silent in her seat, her face stained with tears. Behind them in the sea, her locket sank deeper and deeper, turning and twisting and glimmering in the strange underwater light. From somewhere below, a pair of eyes saw it as it spiralled down. There was a sudden movement, a disturbance and rippling in the water. And from behind a rock on the seabed, a shape emerged and swam towards the strange, shining object . . .

At home Lizzy went to her room, lay down on the bed and cried into her pillow until there were no more tears left. She didn't want tea or supper. Mum brought her a tray and tried to persuade her to eat something, but she refused, and at last Mum decided that the only thing to do was leave her alone until she felt better.

It was dark when Rose came to Lizzy's room. Lizzy was still awake, staring out of the window at the lighthouse beam flashing over the sea. Rose sat down on the ledge beside her sister and put an arm round her shoulders.

'Tell you what,' she said. 'Tomorrow morning, straight after breakfast, we'll go to the beach and look for your locket.'

'T-to the beach?' Lizzy sniffed.

'Yes. The locket's so small and light, there's a chance it'll get washed up on the shore.'

'It won't,' Lizzy said miserably. 'I'm sure it won't.'

Rose shook her gently. 'Don't talk like that! You never know. If we both wish hard enough, we might find it. Worth a try, anyway, yeah?'

Lizzy tried to smile through her sadness. Though they sometimes quarrelled, Rose could be really nice sometimes.

'OK,' she said. 'We'll try. And . . . thanks.'

'Don't be a muppet! Any excuse to go to the beach.' Rose stood up. 'Night, sis.'

She went out, leaving Lizzy feeling a little bit better.

It was still early and there were few people on the beach when the girls arrived the next morning.

'Right,' said Rose briskly, putting her fists on her hips and surveying the golden sand. 'It's such a long beach, better if we start from opposite ends and meet up in the middle. Tell you what, you go from the lighthouse end.' She put on her new sunglasses and twisted her shoulder-length dark hair up in a clip to make herself look older and more sophisticated. 'If I go the other way, I can ask the lifeguards if anything's been handed in.'

Lizzy hid the faintest of smiles. She knew very well that Rose wasn't only interested in finding the locket. But it didn't matter. She was grateful to have help.

As Rose headed towards the spot where the lifeguards were setting up their equipment for the day, Lizzy hurried off in the opposite direction. The lighthouse was about 300 metres away, on a low cliff beyond an outcrop of rocks that marked the end of the beach. Lizzy walked to the outcrop, and then slowly started to retrace her steps. A wavy line of washed-up shells and seaweed showed where the high tide had been, and she sifted through the flotsam with her bare toes, hoping against hope that she would see a tell-tale shimmer of mother-of-pearl.

It was a gorgeous day, with not a cloud in the sky, but Lizzy was hardly aware of it as she searched. Though she did not want to admit it, she was certain, deep down, that there was no real hope of finding her locket. It was too tiny, and the sea too vast. The chances that it would have been carried here by the tide must be millions to one.

Suddenly, though she couldn't explain how, she felt sure that she was being watched. It was a peculiar feeling, like a prickling somewhere in the back of her mind. Lizzy raised her head and looked out to sea.

A single dolphin was swimming not very far from shore. She could see its dorsal fin rising and falling with the swell, and it seemed to be keeping pace with her as she walked. Lizzy stopped – and the dolphin stopped too, rocking gently in the water. This was strange . . . and then an even stranger thought took form in Lizzy's head. It was impossible to tell from this distance, of course, but she was convinced that it was the dolphin with the silver streak on its back. The same one that had swum alongside the boat yesterday and looked at her . . .

On impulse, she turned towards the sea and started to wade into the shallows. However, she was no more than knee deep in the water when the dolphin gave a flip of its tail and was gone. Lizzy shaded her eyes against the sun, looking for another glimpse. But there was no sign of the dolphin.

She felt numb with disappointment. Just for a moment she had wondered if the dolphin had been trying to tell her something. It was crazy, of course. Totally stupid, in fact. Why should it have been the same dolphin? And, even if it was, why should it be interested in her? With a sigh she turned away – and jumped as she came face to face with a boy, not three steps from where she was standing.

They stared at each other. He must have crept up behind her, Lizzy told herself. But where had he come from? He wasn't anywhere in sight a few moments ago. Despite the warm sun, she felt herself shiver. The boy, who wore a T-shirt and swimming shorts, was about her own age. He had jet-black hair and unusually pale skin, and he was wet, as if he had just come out of the sea. He was a complete stranger. But she had the weirdest feeling that she *knew* him.

Then she saw his eyes. They were a very intense blue. In fact, they were exactly the same colour as her own.

The spell that held Lizzy snapped as the boy spoke. He said, 'Hello. Is this what you're looking for?'

He stretched out one hand, palm open, and Lizzy's eyes widened in astonishment.

She gasped, '*My locket!*'

Chapter Three

'Where did you find it?' In her joy Lizzy completely forgot the weird sensation of a few moments ago.

The boy just shrugged. Then his bright blue stare fixed on her searchingly and he asked, 'What's your name?'

'Lizzy. Lizzy Baxter.'

'Oh.' He sounded puzzled – or disappointed? She wasn't sure. 'I'm Kes.'

Lizzy clasped the locket in her hand. 'How did you know it was mine?'

'Easy. I opened it, and I saw that curl of hair inside. Then I saw you, with hair exactly the same colour. I mean, it's pretty unusual, isn't it? So it's got to be your hair in the locket.' He paused. '*Is* it your hair? Or someone else's?'

There was something odd about the way he said 'someone else's', almost as if he very much needed to know the answer to his question.

'I don't know,' Lizzy admitted. 'It might be mine, but . . .' The words tailed off as she realized that he wouldn't be interested in her story.

He *was* interested, though, and his eyes became very alert. 'But what?' he asked eagerly. 'Whose hair is it, if it's not yours?'

Lizzy had never explained about the locket to anyone. Even her school friends didn't know the story; it was just something she didn't talk about. But suddenly words came, and before she even had time to think, she heard herself say, 'I don't know. I'm adopted, you see. The locket was mine when I was a baby, but I don't know anything about my real parents . . .' Abruptly she stopped as she realized what she was doing. Kes was a stranger. She had only just met him. Why was she telling him this?

Kes was staring at her again, and suddenly Lizzy's weird feeling came back. Something was going on. Something strange. Something she didn't understand. It scared her, and that made her angry.

'Why do you want to know?' she demanded. 'It's nothing to do with you! I've never even seen you before, but suddenly you're asking me all these questions. Why? What do you want?'

'Hey, Lizzy!'

The voice startled them both, and Lizzy turned to see Rose heading along the beach towards them. Rose waved – and Kes turned and hurried away along the beach.

'Wait!' Lizzy shouted. But he took no notice. He was running now, splashing through the shallow wavelets towards the rocky cliff where the lighthouse stood. 'What's going on?' Rose asked, reaching Lizzy and stopping. 'Who's that boy?'

'I don't know. But he found my locket.' Lizzy showed it.

'Brilliant!' Rose punched the air. 'I told you, didn't I? If you wished hard enough –'

Lizzy was not listening. She was staring after Kes's running figure, and suddenly she knew she had to go after him. There was a mystery here. She wanted to know what it was. She *had* to know.

'Lizzy?' Rose was startled as with no warning Lizzy started off after Kes. 'Lizzy! Where are you going?'

Lizzy took no notice. She ran as fast as she could, but Kes was faster. He had already reached the rock outcrop at the foot of the cliff and was scrambling up it, and by the time Lizzy reached the rocks he had disappeared over the top.

Lizzy started to climb. Rose had come after her; she too clambered up, and found Lizzy standing on the path at the cliff top. There was no one else in sight.

'Where did he go?' Lizzy asked in a small voice. 'He's just vanished.'

Rose stared around. A short way ahead the path divided. One track curved inland, while the other led to the lighthouse and then on along the coast.

'Whichever way he went,' she said, 'he must be one heck of a fast runner.'

Lizzy didn't answer but only went on staring, as if she couldn't believe what she was – or wasn't – seeing.

'Look,' Rose said at last, uneasily, 'I don't know why he ran off, any more than you do, but you've got your locket back. That's what matters, isn't it?'

Lizzy bit her lip. 'I suppose so . . .'

'Well, then. Come on. Whoever he is, we're not going to catch up with him now.

Let's go back to the beach. He'll probably show up there later, and you can talk to him then.'

Lizzy's shoulders slumped. She followed as Rose led the way back down the rocks. But her face was thoughtful, and every minute or so she looked back over her shoulder, hoping that Kes might reappear. He didn't, of course. But Lizzy was determined that she would find him again. When she did, she would have some questions to ask. And she would want answers.

Lizzy was swimming, but couldn't work out where she was. Beams of light played over her, and the only colours she could see were dim blues and greens that swirled in every direction. Suddenly she realized that she must be under the sea, and immediately she felt frightened. She couldn't hold her breath for long – she must reach the surface, or she would drown!

She tried to turn and swim upwards. But she couldn't do it. Something was holding her back – in fact she was sinking, deeper and deeper, as an invisible force pulled her towards the seabed.

A voice was calling her name. She had never heard the voice before, but it called to her over and over again. There was something eerie about it, almost as if it wasn't human. Lizzy desperately wanted to call back, but she dared not open her mouth.

Now she was no longer underwater; instead she was standing on the beach. She could still hear the eerie voice calling to her, but other voices had joined in, and when she looked towards the sea, she saw dolphins leaping clear of the swell. She was certain that the voices were theirs, and that they were calling to *her*. But why? What were they saying?

Lizzy woke up in fright to find daylight flooding in at her window.

For a few minutes she lay still, as the confusion of dream and reality untangled itself in her mind. It had been so vivid – the voice, the sea, the dolphins – as if it had really happened.

She looked at the clock on her bedside table and saw that it was nearly half past six. The house was very quiet, but in the distance she could hear the early morning bustle of the harbour and the fish market. The beach would be empty at this time of day. If she left a note to say she had gone for a walk and would be back in time for breakfast, Mum and Dad wouldn't worry . . .

She pulled on shorts, sweatshirt and sandals, and slipped quietly out of the house. As she hurried towards the beach she realized that she didn't know why she was doing this. It was just a feeling, an instinct. As if something in her mind was telling her that the dolphins would be there.

They were. As soon as she reached the

long, deserted sweep of the sand she saw
them, close in to shore, leaping and dancing.
A shock went through her as she realized
that the sunlight, the frolicking dolphins,
even the spot where she was standing, were
all *exactly* the same as her dream scene! She
even thought – though she couldn't be sure –
that she could hear the high-pitched
whistling cries that dolphins make, just as, in
the dream, she had heard their voices calling.

Lizzy's pulse began to race with
excitement. Kicking off her sandals she
waded into the sea, splashing out until the
surf was foaming around her thighs. If only
she had brought her wetsuit – she ached to
swim out through the waves to where the
dolphins were. Crazy though the idea might
seem, she was sure they were waiting for her.

Then her heart gave a huge thump as one
of the dolphins turned towards the shore.
Very slowly it started to swim towards her.
The others did not follow, but cruised up

and down, watching. The first dolphin came closer . . .

And behind her, a voice said, 'Lizzy?'

Lizzy whirled round. Kes was standing at the edge of the sea. Again he was wet, as if he had been swimming. They gazed at each other, until a bigger wave than usual broke behind Lizzy and nearly knocked her over. She staggered. Kes splashed through the water to grab her arm and help her regain her balance, and they stumbled together to dry sand.

'I'm sorry,' Kes said.

'Sorry?' Lizzy's heart was thumping again. 'What for?'

'Running away like I did yesterday.' He stared down at his own feet. 'I'm not really supposed to come here. But . . . I had to see you again.'

She swallowed. 'Why?'

There was a long silence. Then Kes said in a low, quiet voice, 'It was your locket. You see . . . my sister was taken away when we were babies. She had a locket just like yours. I was too young to remember, but my mother told me about it. And when you said what you did about not knowing who your real parents are . . .'

A strange, tingling sensation started to creep up Lizzy's spine. She tried to find her voice, but the words wouldn't form properly and all she could do was stammer, 'Do you . . . I mean, are you trying to . . .?'

Kes's eyes were very intense. Then he said, 'I think I'm your brother.'

Chapter Four

Lizzy began to shake and couldn't make it stop. This was impossible! She was still dreaming, she had to be! In a minute she would wake up.

'Y-your parents . . .' She heard her own voice, but it seemed to be coming from far away. 'They . . . where are they?'

'I live with my mother,' said Kes.

She didn't believe any of this. She *couldn't* believe it. 'Where?' she whispered.

'I . . . can't tell you.'

Suddenly Lizzy's self-control snapped, and she screamed at him. 'What do you mean?

You've got to tell me! You can't say what – what you just said, and then – then –'

'I can't!'

'*Why not?*' Lizzy yelled.

Kes glanced quickly from left to right, as if he were looking for a way of escape. Then he said, 'Because you'd never believe me.'

And before she could do anything, he turned and ran away as he had done before.

'Wait!' Lizzy shrieked desperately. 'Come back!'

Kes just kept running, heading for the rock outcrop again. This time, though, Lizzy didn't hesitate. She sprinted after him, hair flying, feet thudding on the sand. He was halfway up the rocks when she reached them, and she scrabbled after him as fast as she could. The rocks were covered with mussels and barnacles, which hurt her feet, but she didn't care. All that mattered was to catch up with Kes.

By the time he reached the top and

disappeared, Lizzy was only a few metres behind. She hauled herself over the cliff edge and scrambled upright in time to see him hurrying along the outer path, towards the lighthouse. She paused just long enough to take two deep breaths, and then gave chase again.

The lighthouse was bigger than it had looked from a distance, looming over Lizzy as she neared it. Its bulk blocked her view of Kes now, but he must still be on the path. She ran round the landward side of the tower – and slid to a halt.

The path ahead of her was empty. Kes had gone.

Gasping, Lizzy stared at the deserted path in disbelief. Where *was* he? There was no way he could have run fast enough to be out of sight, yet somehow he had done it. Unless . . . She looked at the lighthouse. There was only one possibility. Kes must be hiding on the other side of it, waiting for her to run on along the path before he doubled back. *OK,* she thought. *Then he's in for a surprise!*

Very quietly, holding her breath, she began to edge round the curve of the lighthouse wall. Just a little bit further, and –

'Caught you!' she yelled, making a rush to the far side.

There was nobody there. Only the silent lighthouse and the cliff edge beyond it, with the sea rising and falling and slapping against the rocks below.

Confused, Lizzy turned in a circle, half expecting Kes to jump out and say that the whole thing had been a joke. Inside, though, she knew that there was nothing funny about this. *I think I'm your brother.* He had meant it. He hadn't been lying, she was absolutely certain. He believed it. But was it true? *Could* it be true? And what was the mystery about his mother, and where they lived? She had to know!

Movement in the sea caught her eye.

Looking down, she saw the dolphins again. They had followed her, and now they were swimming in circles just off the headland. Above the noise of the tide Lizzy heard their high-pitched whistles echoing from the cliff face, and it seemed to her that they were trying to tell her something. A wild thought came to her – could they see Kes? Had he climbed down the rocks, out of her sight but visible to them?

Moving to the cliff edge Lizzy leaned cautiously over. She couldn't see anyone, but there were so many folds and humps in the rock where Kes could easily be hiding. She licked her lips. Could she climb down? She was pretty sure-footed, and it didn't look *too* difficult. Maybe if she went just a few metres, until she could see round that first outcrop . . .

Very slowly and cautiously she began to feel her way down. It wasn't that bad; in fact it was no harder than the climb up here from the beach; it just looked worse because the sea was below her instead of firm sand, and its movement made her dizzy. All right . . . She had a good handhold; if she wedged her right foot *here*, then she could put her left foot *there*, and –

Her foot slipped, her body twisting round before she could stop it, and suddenly, horrifyingly, she lost her grip and started to slither downwards. Lizzy screamed and clutched desperately for another handhold. But there was nothing to grasp. She was sliding faster down the rocks, knees and elbows scraping painfully – the world seemed to turn upside down as blue-green water rose to meet her, and with another scream she plunged into the sea.

She hit the surface hard. Water closed over her head and the noise of the tide filled her ears, like the roar when an express train enters a tunnel. Salt stung her eyes, mouth and nose – then suddenly she burst up into light and air, to find herself bobbing on the

swell with the cliff slope just a few metres
away.

But a few metres were more than enough.
However good a swimmer Lizzy might be, the
indoor pools she was used to were totally
different from the surge and rush and sheer
power of the ocean. The current was already
carrying her away. She tried to strike out
against it but it was far too strong for her. She
began to panic, her swimming strokes turning
into a splashing struggle as she fought to reach
the rocks. The tide pulled at her, each rise and
fall taking her further from safety. She couldn't
fight it, she would drown –

'Help!' Lizzy cried, spluttering as a wave
broke against her face. 'Help!'

Through water-blurred eyes she saw
something heading straight for her. For a
terrifying moment she thought she was about
to be thrown on to a submerged rock – then
her vision cleared, and she saw the sleek
shape of a dolphin. Silver glinted in a long

streak down its back, and with a cry Lizzy
stretched out a frantic hand towards it. Her
fingers grasped its dorsal fin; a second
dolphin was there too, and with her other
hand she grabbed a tight hold of its flipper.
She had read stories of dolphins helping
human swimmers in trouble – now she knew
that the stories were true. The dolphins were
rescuing her! They were –

Lizzy's joy turned to horror, for with no
warning the dolphins dived, pulling her with
them under the water. She struggled wildly,
letting go of the fins and trying to swim
away. But the dolphins closed in on her,
wedging her tightly between their smooth
bodies. Now there was a third dolphin
above, pressing her downwards. Like the
invisible force in her dream they were taking
her deeper and deeper. Colours swirled
around her, green and blue and indigo; her
ears were drumming, her lungs felt as if they
must burst. *She had to breathe!*

Unable to stop herself, she opened her
mouth –

And breathed.

Lizzy knew that this couldn't be happening
to her. She was human! She couldn't breathe
underwater, like a fish! It was another
dream; she was asleep in her own bed, and
soon she would wake up – or maybe, she
thought, almost calm now, this was what
drowning was like. A kind of trance or
hallucination. Not frightening, but gentle and
beautiful. For the underwater world was very
beautiful indeed. Light played in fascinating
patterns, brighter above her, darker beneath.
A fish with shining scales of blue, green,
purple and orange swam past, and a shoal of
tiny wriggling sand eels darted across her
path. Then below she saw the smooth, pale
sand of the seabed. Rocks were scattered on
it, with sea anemones anchored to them like
exotic flowers, their tentacles waving lazily in
the current. As though enchanted by some

strange, vague spell, Lizzy gazed dreamily at it as the dolphins guided her down towards the sand. The water was wonderfully clear, and though she knew she should be feeling cold, somehow she was warm instead.

The dolphin to her right – the one with the silver streak – was whistling now, or at least she thought it was. Certainly she could hear a sound, carrying through the water, which gave it a strange, echoey quality. Was the dolphin talking to her? She thought it was, though she couldn't understand what it was trying to say. Then from somewhere ahead came an answering whistle, and moments later a dim shape emerged from among the rocks a short way off. For a few moments Lizzy did not recognize the figure as it rose from the seabed and swam towards her. But when she did the shock was so great that her trance snapped and her eyes widened in amazement.

The figure coming to meet them was Kes. As he arrived, the three dolphins veered away, leaving Lizzy suspended in the water. Kes smiled at her, but she could only stare back in utter bewilderment as her thoughts ran wild. *We're under the sea. We're breathing! I'm not dreaming, or drowning – this is REAL!*

Then Kes smiled and said, 'Welcome home.'

A stream of bubbles came from his mouth as he spoke. Lizzy's own mouth worked, and she saw similar bubbles drift past her face.

'I . . .' She tried her voice, and found that she, too, could speak. 'I don't . . . understand . . .'

Kes smiled again, and then put a finger to his lips. 'Shh! It's all right. There's nothing to be scared of. This is my world – and it's yours too. It always has been.' Reaching out, he took hold of her hand. 'Come and see.'

Chapter Five

All Lizzy's common sense told her that this couldn't possibly be happening. She was an ordinary human girl, no different from anyone else. Humans didn't live under the sea. They couldn't. Yet here she was, breathing water as easily as she breathed air, swimming with Kes far, far down beneath the waves. And Kes himself – what was he?

Her mind was so crowded with questions that she didn't know where to begin asking. Besides, everything here was so strange and beautiful that there was no time to ask, in case she missed one of the wonderful sights. She would never have thought that seaweed could look like a forest. She had never realized how many different kinds of fish swam here, of every colour and shape imaginable. She could never have believed that the undersea light was like a hundred sparkling rainbows.

They were drifting over an outcrop of rock, where tiny crabs scurried among the jewel-coloured anemones, when she saw a glimmer of grey ahead. Moments later the dolphin with the silver streak was swimming with them. It dived under Lizzy and surged over her, rolling in the water like a huge friendly dog playing a game. As it swam past, Lizzy saw the look in its eye. There was humour and mischief there, and for a moment Lizzy almost expected it to wink at her.

The dolphin gave a series of whistles, and Kes grinned. 'Her name is Arhans,' he said, bubbles streaming from his mouth again. 'And she says she likes you very much.'

'Can you understand her?' Lizzy was astonished.

'Oh, yes. You can learn too. It isn't difficult. All you have to do is listen, and you'll find it will start to happen.'

'How? Other humans can't talk to dolphins. Why should I be able to?'

'Ah . . .' Kes's expression became more serious. 'Yes, I . . . I suppose I should explain everything.' He stopped swimming and let himself drift on the current, then looked around him, a little uneasily, Lizzy thought. 'I don't want to talk about it here, though. We should go back to shore. But before we do –'

He reached behind him, and for the first time Lizzy noticed something slung over his back. It was like a shoulder bag, but it appeared to be made from woven seaweed. Kes rummaged inside it, and drew out a large empty shell with a twisting spiral shape.

'It's for you,' he said. 'From my collection.'

'Oh, it's lovely! Thank you!' She reached out to take it, but he shook his head.

'There's more to it than that. I'll give it to you when we're on shore, and tell you about it. Come on – it's time we went back.'

He set off, curving up towards the surface. Lizzy hesitated, but Arhans chittered and nudged gently at her, as if urging her to follow. She had the feeling that the dolphin was reassuring her. Slowly she began to move, finning the water with her hands and feet as she turned away from the incredible undersea world and headed back to shore.

They surfaced at the beach. There was still no one around. Even the lifeguards hadn't arrived yet, which meant it must still be very early, though the sun was already warm on Lizzy's skin as she waded unsteadily out on to dry sand. Water streamed from her hair and clothes and she could feel herself shaking, not with cold, but with shock. *Had* it happened? Now, on dry land, she could hardly believe it.

Confused, she looked back at the sea. Arhans was gone. The dolphin had swum away as Lizzy found her feet in the shallows, and now there was no sign that she had ever been there at all. But Kes was with her, standing knee-deep in the water and swaying with the rush and pull of the waves. For an awful moment Lizzy feared he would dive back into the sea and disappear like Arhans. Instead, though, he waded to her. He was still holding the shell he had taken from his shoulder bag.

'I'm sorry,' he said, 'but I couldn't tell you the truth before. You wouldn't have believed me. You had to find out for yourself.'

Lizzy swallowed. 'You mean that I could . . . can . . .'

'Live under the sea. Yes. You've always been able to.'

Fear rose in Lizzy and she flared up at him. 'That's not true! It's crazy! I've never been able to do it before!'

'You have. It's just that you'd forgotten.' Kes nodded over his shoulder. 'The dolphins knew who you were as soon as they saw you. So they showed you, and you remembered.'

Lizzy stared at him. She was shivering more than ever but tried not to let it show. 'What do you mean, they *knew*?' she demanded. '*Who* do they think I am?'

Kes's bright blue eyes gazed deeply into hers. 'I told you,' he said. 'You're my sister. We don't look alike, but we're twins. Arhans told me you had come back. Then when I found your locket, and saw you hunting for it on the beach . . .' His voice suddenly became unsteady. 'You see . . . you look just like our mother.'

Lizzy's lower lip started to tremble and she had an awful feeling that she was about to burst into tears. She desperately, desperately wanted to believe what Kes was telling her. But could she? *Dared* she? Or was this all a strange dream, from which she would suddenly wake up?

With immense effort she got herself under control. 'If I *am* your sister,' she whispered, 'why was I adopted? Why did your mother' – she couldn't bring herself to say *our* mother – 'give me away?'

It was Kes's turn to flare up. 'She didn't! You were stolen! Our father went looking for you, but he never came back and –' He stopped suddenly as he saw the look of utter shock on Lizzy's face. 'Didn't you know?' he finished.

'No, of course not! How could I have done? *No one* knows anything about me, except that I was found abandoned. They couldn't trace my family, so I got taken to a children's home, and then the Baxters adopted me.' She was crying now. 'I don't know what to think. I don't know what to believe!'

'I'm your brother,' said Kes gently. 'You can believe that.' And she saw that he was nearly crying too.

Yet even through the massive surge of emotion, something else was whirling in Lizzy's mind. Humans couldn't live underwater. But she and Kes could. Which must mean . . .

Taking a deep breath Lizzy said, 'Kes . . . what are we? Are we people – I mean real people, human people? Or –' She couldn't finish.

Kes stared down at the sand. 'Our father's human. His name's Jack; that's all I know about him. He went away when I was too young to remember.'

'To search for me?'

Kes nodded.

'And . . . and your mother . . .?'

He gave a funny little half-laugh. 'She's called Morvyr,' he said. There was a long pause. Then: 'She's a mermaid.'

Lizzy stared at him. '*What?*'

Kes shrugged. 'She's –'

'I heard! But there are no such things as mermaids!'

He shrugged again. 'That's what most people on land think. They're wrong, though.' His head came up again and he looked at her challengingly. 'Like you said, humans can't live underwater. But mermaids can.'

They held each other's gazes for a few moments more. Then with no warning it all became too much for Lizzy. She felt her legs giving way under her, and helplessly she sat down with a *crump* on the sand and started to laugh. There was nothing funny about her laughter; it was more like hysterics. But she couldn't make it stop, and tears were mixed in with it too, so that she ended up covering her mouth with her hands and hiccupping violently.

'Sorry,' Kes said. 'But you asked.'

That *did* strike Lizzy as funny, and she began laughing again. Kes came over and awkwardly patted her shoulder. 'Sorry,' he repeated. 'It was all my fault.'

'Wh-what was?' Lizzy gasped.

'Shocking you like that. I really *am* sorry . . . I wanted to tell you the truth when I first saw you today, but I lost my nerve. That's why I ran away. I didn't mean you to fall in the sea the way you did.'

Lizzy looked up at him. 'But the dolphins had other ideas, didn't they?' She smiled to show she wasn't angry, and Kes smiled too.

'I s'pose they did. They're like that; 'specially Arhans. She's very wise.'

'So she lured me, and they showed me what I could do.' Lizzy's eyes clouded. 'What I am . . .'

Kes knelt down beside her. He still had the shell, and he pressed it into her hand. 'Hold it to your ear,' he said. 'Tell me what you can hear.'

Lizzy knew the old stories about hearing the sea in a shell. She and Rose had often done it on family holidays. Never in Cornwall, though. At least, not until now . . . She took the shell and pressed it against her ear. A hissing-roaring sound filled her head, like waves breaking on shore. Then Kes said, 'Listen harder,' and to her astonishment the sounds started to change. The sea noise was still there, but mingling with it were what seemed like blurry, murmuring voices.

'It's the dolphins talking,' said Kes. 'They're happy and excited, because you've come back.'

'It's beautiful!' Lizzy whispered in wonder.

'It'll take time for you to tune in, but when you do you'll be able to talk to them when you're on land. And to me.' Kes smiled. 'All you have to do is hold the shell to your ear, and we'll be with you.'

The roar of a motor vehicle's engine suddenly broke the spell, and Lizzy turned her head to see the lifeguards' 4x4 trundling across the sand. Their day's work was starting – Mum and Dad must be up by now. She'd meant to leave them a note, but in her hurry to get to the beach she had forgotten. What if they went to her room and found her missing?

'I must go!' She scrambled to her feet. 'My parents will start worrying!'

'Can't you stay a bit longer?' Kes pleaded.

'No, I've got to get back!'

'When can you come again?'

She thought quickly. Mum wanted to go shopping in Penzance today, to buy things for the new house. She and Rose had said they would go too. She couldn't get out of it, or it would look suspicious. 'Tomorrow,' she

said. 'Early morning, here on the beach.'
There was a lump in her throat. She tried to
gulp it back but it wouldn't go. 'Will you tell
your mother about me?'

'Yes!' said Kes. 'She'll so much want to see
you! But she doesn't go too near land. It's
difficult for her. So I'll have to take you to
her.' He paused. 'Will you come?'

Lizzy's eyes were shining. 'Yes, please!'
Then suddenly a new thought came to her.
'Kes . . . the children's home called me
Elizabeth – Lizzy – because no one knew my
real name.' She swallowed again. 'Do *you*
know what my real name is?'

'Of course I do.' Kes smiled. 'It's Tegenn.'

Tegenn. It sounded so strange, so
unfamiliar. *But it's me*, Lizzy thought. *It's my
real name . . .*

She couldn't wait for tomorrow to come.

Chapter Six

By the time her house came in sight, everything was starting to feel unreal to Lizzy. She was giddy with a mixture of shock, excitement and confusion, as if her mind simply wasn't big enough to take in all that had happened and make sense of it. Going round to the back of the house, she cautiously eased the back door open and peered into the kitchen. There was no one there, and no noises that she could hear. Maybe Mum and Dad weren't up yet.

She glided up the stairs as silently as a ghost and went to her bedroom. There was a mirror on the table, and she sat down and stared at her reflection. Her own face stared back; round, fair-skinned, with a snub nose ('a cute little button' Dad called it) and a sprinkling of freckles. Her wavy blonde hair was a mess; even though it was soaking wet it bounced and curled round her face in its usual unruly way. It would never do what she wanted it to, and even though she had recently had it cut quite short, it still refused to behave. *You look just like our mother*, Kes had said. Lizzy found that hard to believe. But her eyes . . . oh, yes, they were exactly like Kes's. Such a bright blue, like the sky and the sea on a summer day . . .

A seagull landed on the roof above her room and started to scream raucously. That noise would wake Mum and Dad – if she didn't hurry up, they'd see her before she could get changed! Hastily Lizzy pulled off her clothes. The sun and wind had dried them a bit as she ran home, but they were still wet enough to be a problem. She found a plastic carrier bag, stuffed them into it, and then pushed the bag out of sight under her bed. She would put them in the washing machine later. If she did it now, everyone would be suspicious. Then, grabbing some dry things, she hurried to the bathroom. A shower would explain her wet hair, and with luck no one would be any the wiser.

Coming out of the bathroom after her shower, she bumped into Rose.

'Oh, it was you making all that noise in there,' Rose said, and yawned. 'You woke me up! What on earth are you doing showering at this hour?'

'Sorry,' said Lizzy. 'I just thought I'd get up early, as it's such a lovely day.'

'Is it?' Rose yawned again. 'I haven't looked.' She was not an early riser. Mum usually had to call her at least four times before she tottered sleepily down to breakfast. 'Oh, well,' she added grudgingly, 'I

suppose I might as well make a cup of tea.
Fat chance I'll get back to sleep if you're
going to thunder around like a herd of
elephants.'

Lizzy grinned and went to her bedroom,
where she opened the curtains. Rose followed
her, blinking at the bright daylight. She
peered at herself in Lizzy's mirror, grimaced
and then sniffed. 'What's that smell?'

'What smell?' Lizzy had not noticed
anything.

'Sort of briny. Like the sea. You haven't
been bringing buckets of water back from
the beach, have you?'

'Don't be silly, of course I haven't!' It was
her wet clothes, of course. Lizzy looked
furtively at the floor by her bed to make sure
the bag was out of sight. But Rose had
stopped looking in the mirror and had seen
something else.

'Oh, it must be this.' She crossed the room
and picked up the spiral shell that Kes had

given to Lizzy. 'Wow, it's enormous! Where did you get it?'

'I – found it on the beach,' Lizzy lied. Her heart had started to beat uncomfortably fast.

Rose grinned. 'Remember when we used to hold shells against our ears, to see if we could hear the sea? Bet you can hear it with this one!'

She made to put the shell to her own ear, but Lizzy darted forward and snatched it out of her hand. 'No, don't!' she said.

Rose stared at her in surprise. 'I won't damage it.'

'I – I know . . . It's just that – well . . .' Thinking frantically, Lizzy babbled the first thing that came to mind. 'It's the sort of thing little kids do, isn't it? And we're not little kids now. I mean . . .'

The words tailed off. Rose was looking at her curiously. Then she shrugged. 'OK, suit yourself. If you don't want me to touch it, I won't.'

'It isn't that,' said Lizzy awkwardly. 'It's just . . .'

'Oh, forget it. You're nuts, that's all. I'll make that tea. Do you want some?'

The lifeguards were still busy setting up their equipment for the day, so they didn't notice Kes as he waded back into the water and swam out to sea. He looked for Arhans, but she was nowhere to be seen. That was odd, he thought. The dolphin had been so excited about finding his long-lost sister that he had expected her to stay around. Oh, well. Perhaps she had already gone back to his mother, to tell her the news. Kes hoped not, because *he* wanted to be the one to tell it. He wanted to see Morvyr's face!

Past the breakers, he dived and swam fast under the surface, heading for his home further westward along the coast. He felt excited too, even more excited than Arhans and her friends. Tegenn – Lizzy – his own sister! It was the most wonderful thing that had ever happened to Kes, and all he wanted was to reach the underwater cave where he and Morvyr lived. Before long he saw a sea-forest ahead of him: long, brown strands of oar-weed that swayed in the current like flowing hair. He swam towards it and pushed his way in among the waving strands. The weed stroked him gently as he passed. It was quite difficult to swim through, and he often wondered why his mother had chosen to live here instead of in a more open place. He had asked her, many times, but she only said, 'When you're older, you'll understand.'

Crabs scurried among the weed, and a large blue-black lobster waggled its feelers at Kes as he passed. He called jokingly, 'Don't go too near any lobster pots!' but the lobster didn't answer. It was too old and too wise to be worried about human fishermen. A small octopus came out of the forest's depths and swam alongside him. It was curious, but Kes did not want to stop and talk. All he wanted was to get home, to see his mother and tell her everything.

He emerged from the forest and there it was, a cave hollowed into the rocky coast on the seabed. Kes could see the curtain of seaweed that covered the entrance, surrounded by anemones that waved their bright-coloured tentacles in the current. He put on a burst of speed – then suddenly there was a swirling of water inside the cave, the weed curtain parted and his mother emerged.

Morvyr had white-blonde hair that flowed behind her, and eyes the grey of a stormy sea. Her hair was exactly the same colour as Lizzy's. But instead of human legs, she had a long, green tail that shimmered with silvery scales, like the tail of a fish.

'Kes, where have you been?' The mermaid sounded agitated.

'I've been ashore,' said Kes. 'Mother, I –'

'How many times have I told you not to go off on your own without telling me?'

'I'm sorry – but Arhans was with me, and she knew it was all right. Mother –'

Morvyr didn't let him finish. 'You're home now; that's all that matters. Kes, I have to go. Not for long; I'll be back tomorrow if all's well.'

'Go?' asked Kes. 'Where?'

'To the Queen.'

He was surprised and dismayed. 'The Queen? What does she want?'

'Gifts. One of her messengers came.' Morvyr shivered. 'She has summoned all the merfolk from hereabouts to a gathering-place past Land's End. She demands tribute.'

'The next tribute isn't due for another three new moons!' said Kes.

'She says the last one wasn't enough, and she wants more.'

'That isn't fair!'

'I know. But what can we do? We daren't refuse. You know what happens if anyone disobeys her. She uses her powers to punish them. And we can't fight that kind of magic.' Morvyr looked at a bag made from woven seaweed that was slung over her shoulder. 'I only hope I have enough to please her. There's mother-of-pearl, and a picking of the rare seaweed that only grows far out in the deep water, and some silver lures that human fishermen lost from their boats. And . . .' Her voice caught suddenly. 'And my coral necklace.'

'Mother! You don't mean the one that great-grandfather made, with the corals he brought from the South Seas?'

Morvyr nodded sadly. 'I have no choice, Kes. There isn't enough time to find more things to give her.'

'It's not fair!' Kes cried. 'The Queen's selfish and greedy – I *hate* her!'

'Shh!' Morvyr glanced around nervously.

'You mustn't ever say things like that. What if one of her spies was nearby and heard you? Now, I *must* go. The Queen will be angry if anyone is late.'

'Mother!' Kes said desperately as she began to swim away. 'There's something I've got to tell you –'

'It will have to wait.'

'It can't wait!' Kes drew a deep breath. 'I've found Tegenn!'

Instantly Morvyr stopped and turned round. '*What?*'

Kes swallowed. 'I've found my sister. She lives on shore. In the town, with a human family.'

Morvyr's eyes widened and she stared at him. 'It can't be true . . .'

'It *is* true! She's called Lizzy now, but her hair is just like yours, and her eyes are the same colour as mine. She can breathe underwater, the same as we can. And she's still got her locket.'

'Oh, Kes . . .' His mother's mouth began to tremble. Forgetting all about the Queen's summons, she came back to him and grasped his arms. 'Tell me! Tell me everything!'

Kes opened his mouth, but before he could even begin his story, they both heard other voices calling.

'Morvyr! Aren't you ready yet?'

From the weed forest three mermaids and two mermen appeared. They all had woven bags like Morvyr's, and they were very agitated.

'Come on, Morvyr!' urged an older mermaid with long, silver hair.

'We must hurry,' added another, 'or the Queen will punish us!'

'Kes, I *have* to go!' said Morvyr in distress. 'Our friends are right – we daren't risk angering the Queen.'

'But Tegenn –'

'*Hush!*' She put a finger to her lips. 'Don't say her name out loud. Don't say anything to *anyone*. This must be our secret until I come back.'

'But I promised to meet her tomorrow morning.'

'Then go, tell her where I've gone, and that I'll see her when I return. Oh, Kes . . .'

'Come *on*, Morvyr!' cried the others.

'I'm coming!' she called back. 'Tell her, Kes. Tell her! And take care of yourself!'

With a flick of her tail she streaked away to join the others. Within moments they had all disappeared among the curtains of oar-weed.

Kes was still staring at the spot where his mother had vanished when Arhans arrived. The dolphin chittered sympathetically, and Kes stroked her smooth head. 'I *hate* the Queen!' he said angrily. Arhans chittered again, and he sighed. 'I know. I shouldn't say that in case anyone's listening – it could get me into a lot of trouble. But I was so looking forward to Tegenn meeting Mother tomorrow, and now it's all spoiled!'

Arhans nuzzled him, whistling, and reluctantly he nodded. 'You're right, I suppose,' he said. 'It's only another day. And at least I can see Tegenn and talk to her in the meantime.' At last he managed a small smile. 'I suppose I ought to call her Lizzy really, oughtn't I? It's the name she knows. Though it sounds very strange to me.'

The weed forest was quiet now; everyone had gone. Kes sighed again. He might as well go inside the cave, he thought, and wait until tomorrow. There wasn't much else to do.

The seaweed curtain parted as he pushed at it, and he drifted gently into his home. It was a very different kind of home to anything found on land. The cave had a low ceiling but it was quite large, and the sand of the floor was so pale that it was more silver than yellow. Weed of many different colours and shapes grew from the walls; flat green sea lettuces, delicate red dulse, leathery brown clumps of wrack with their bulbous

80

air-bladders, which Kes had loved to burst when he was little. A shoal of small fish wriggled out of his path, then flipped up to the roof and hid among the crevices where limpets and striped periwinkles moved slowly. To one side of the floor was a driftwood table. It had been made by Kes's father, and it was the only thing in the cave that resembled human furniture. To the other side there was a large natural alcove in the rock, covered with a seaweed blanket. This was where Morvyr slept. Kes's own sleeping area was reached through a short tunnel at the back of the cave, and he swam into the tunnel and through it to the chamber beyond.

His room was small, and cluttered with all the treasures that Kes had gathered since he was old enough to swim on his own. As well as coloured pebbles and shells of all shapes and sizes, there was a length of rope, a bright orange fishing float, a child's blue plastic spade, the top of a vacuum flask – all sorts of things lost by land-dwellers, which had been carried away by the sea. But most precious of all to Kes were his shells, and now he settled on the sandy floor and began to sort through the collection.

He wondered where Lizzy kept the shell he had given her, and tried to imagine what her own special room must be like. Maybe she was looking at the shell now, holding it to her ear . . . Kes reached out and picked up another shell. Would he hear her, if he listened? He so much wanted to talk to her again and tell her what had happened. But then with a sigh he put the shell down again. His mother had told him he must be patient, and she was right. Tomorrow, he thought. He would see Lizzy again tomorrow.

He put the shell back and let the current carry him slowly to his own sleeping couch.

Chapter Seven

Lizzy got through the rest of that day in a daze. It was just as well that she had the shopping trip with Mum and Rose to concentrate on. The ride in the car to Penzance, then the distraction of all the different shops, took her thoughts away from the incredible things that had happened to her just a few hours ago. By the time they got back home she was much calmer, and was even beginning to wonder if she could have dreamed the whole thing.

But when she went to her bedroom, there was the shell on the shelf where she had left it. And outside on the line were her damp clothes, which she had washed and hung up before they left for Penzance . . .

'You look a bit peaky, love,' Mum said after dinner. 'Are you feeling all right? You haven't been out in the sun too much, have you?'

Lizzy shook her head. 'No, I'm fine. A bit tired, that's all.'

'Lizzy's not a born shopper, that's her trouble,' said Rose. She was feeling very pleased because Mum had given her the money to buy two pairs of shoes and a shoulder bag.

Dad said, 'Just as well. *Two* of you spending money like water would finish Mum and me off!' He grinned to show he didn't really mean it, and Rose made a mock swipe at him.

'Well, if you're feeling all right tomorrow, Lizzy,' said Mum, 'I thought maybe we could all go somewhere for the day. Start exploring Cornwall.'

Lizzy looked at her in dismay. 'Oh, no! I can't – I mean –' She swallowed, realizing what she had been about to say. 'I'd rather go to the beach,' she finished lamely.

Mum looked huffed and started to say that there were loads of beaches to choose from wherever they went. But Rose came to Lizzy's rescue.

'Oh, Mum, can't we go another day? I've got something to do.'

'What?' Mum asked.

Rose's face flushed slightly. 'I . . . er . . . promised to meet someone.'

'Did you now?' Dad put in. 'And who might that be?'

'His name's Paul.' Rose looked at them both a bit guiltily. 'He's really great. He lives around here. His dad's a fisherman, with his own boat.'

'And how old is he?' Dad asked.

'Seventeen. You'd like him, honestly you would. He's –'

Mum burst out laughing. 'Stop questioning her, Mark!' she said to Dad. 'She's not too young to have a boyfriend. Anyway, I seem to remember I was her age when I met you!'

She and Rose both started to tease Dad. Lizzy did not join in, but she felt very relieved. It looked as if Mum's idea of going somewhere tomorrow wasn't going to come to anything. Which meant she would be free to meet Kes.

Lizzy went to bed early that night. She was tired and she wanted to get away from everyone and have some time on her own. In her room she picked up the spiral shell, turning it over and over in her hands. She was half afraid to hold it to her ear, not because of what she might hear, but in case she heard nothing at all. At last, though, she gathered her courage.

She heard the gentle, far-away hissing-roaring that she had heard before. A science teacher at school had once said it was only an echo of her own pulse inside her head, but Lizzy knew in her heart that it *was* the sea. Then, as she listened, something else mingled with the sound. The voices of the dolphins . . . If she concentrated very hard, she liked to believe that she could almost understand what they were saying.

Slowly Lizzy put the shell down, then moved to her window seat and gazed out over the rooftops and beyond the darkening harbour. The sea had a shimmery look under the moonlight, and she knew that somewhere out there were Kes and the dolphins. Tomorrow, they would be waiting for her.

The lighthouse beam moved slowly over the water and vanished on its circling round. Leaving her window and curtains open to the night, Lizzy climbed into bed and closed her eyes.

To her own surprise she slept soundly, and when she woke up the sun was streaming into her room. Hastily throwing on some clothes, she rushed downstairs. Here was another surprise: Rose, showered and dressed and bolting a bowl of muesli at the kitchen table.

'Ha! Beat you to it!' Rose said triumphantly. 'Are you going to the beach?'

'Er . . . yes.' Lizzy started to worry. 'Why?'

'Because I might see you there later. I'm meeting Paul, and we'll probably go for a swim as the weather's so gorgeous.'

'Up early *and* swimming?' said Dad, looking up from the morning paper. 'I don't believe it! This Paul must be having a good influence on you!'

Rose stuck her tongue out at him. 'Fishermen always get up early,' she said.

'I thought you said Paul's still at school?'

'Well, yes. But he goes fishing on his dad's boat sometimes, so he's a fisherman too.' Rose finished her last spoonful and jumped to her feet. 'Anyway, I haven't got time to hang around nattering. I'll see you lazy lot later!'

She snatched up her new bag and whirled out of the door, the bright blue of a tankini showing under her thin cotton shirt.

'Well, well,' said Dad, grinning. 'Our Rose is a reformed character! How about you, Lizzy, love? Are you meeting any friends on the beach?'

'No, Dad. I'm just going swimming.' Lizzy didn't like lying, and had a horrible feeling that her face was turning bright red. Luckily, though, Dad was looking at the paper again. *If only he knew*, she thought. And Rose would be on the beach. That could be tricky – she'd better get there as quickly as she could, and meet Kes before her sister turned up.

'Where's Mum?' she asked.

'Having a lie-in.'

'Oh, right. I'll go, then, if that's OK.'

'Don't you want any breakfast?'

'Er . . . not really. I'm not hungry yet and,

anyway, you shouldn't swim straight after eating. I'll take a cheese roll and some fruit and have them later.'

To her relief Dad didn't argue. Lizzy ran back upstairs, hastily tidied her room and left the house. When she reached the beach she saw that it was already quite crowded. There were people in the sea, people spreading themselves out with rugs and windbreaks and beach-bags, and the familiar 4x4 was parked on the sand, with one of the lifeguards sitting on the roof and scanning the water through binoculars. As she pulled her wetsuit on over her swimsuit, Lizzy looked around for Kes, but she couldn't see him. She only hoped Rose wouldn't show up before he did, or she might start asking awkward questions.

'Lizzy!' said a voice behind her.

Lizzy started and swung round. Kes was there. He wore swimming shorts, but his hair wasn't wet.

'You made me jump!'

'I've been waiting ages – you said you'd be early.'

'I couldn't get away before.' Lizzy did not want to admit that she had overslept. She took a deep breath. 'Did you tell your mother?'

'Yes. She's thrilled, Lizzy. Honestly, I've never seen her so excited. But there's a problem. She can't meet you today.'

Lizzy's face fell. 'Why not?' she asked.

'She's had to go away,' said Kes. 'Only for a day or so, but there was nothing she could do about it.'

'Is something wrong?'

He frowned. 'Well, no, but . . .'

'Hi, you two!' called a voice, and they turned to see Rose, with a boy in tow, heading towards them.

'Oh, no!' Lizzy hissed. 'It's my sister – she said she was coming here, but I thought we could avoid her.' She thought quickly. 'Look, don't say anything except "hello" and "nice to meet you" and that sort of thing. I'll do the rest of the talking.'

Rose and her companion reached them, and Rose beamed at Kes. 'Hi. I'm Rose, Lizzy's sister.'

'This is my friend Kes,' said Lizzy quickly. 'He's the one who found my locket.'

'Of course! I thought I'd seen you somewhere before.' Rose grinned. 'You were too shy to hang around last time, though.'

'He just had to get home, that was all,' said Lizzy defensively.

'Sure. Anyway, this is *my* friend, Paul Treleaven. If you live round here, Kes, I expect you two know each other?'

Kes shook his head, and Paul said, 'Don't think so. Hi, Kes. Hi, Lizzy. Nice to meet you.'

He had darker brown hair than Rose's, hazel eyes, a suntan and a friendly smile. Lizzy liked him immediately, and she liked him even more when he added, 'Come on, Rose, I don't suppose these two want us around. They've got their own things to do. Let's go and swim.'

'OK.' Rose looked at Kes again. 'Lizzy will have to bring you to our house some time. Come and have tea, and meet Mum and Dad.'

'Er . . . yes,' said Kes. 'Th-thanks . . .'

Rose raised her eyebrows at Lizzy in a way that promised plenty of teasing later on, and she and Paul walked away along the beach.

Lizzy let out a long breath of relief. 'I'm glad they've gone! Kes, what's happened with your mother? What is it she's got to do that's more important than meeting me?'

'I said, she didn't want to go, she *had* to.' Kes flicked a glance over his shoulder. 'Let's find somewhere quieter, and I'll explain.'

'The lighthouse?' Lizzy suggested.

They hurried to the end of the beach and climbed up the rocks to the deserted lighthouse. There, Kes told her about the summons from the Queen.

'Who's the Queen?' Lizzy wanted to know. 'Another mermaid?'

'Yes. Her name's Taran. She's very powerful, and everyone's afraid of her.' He frowned. 'She sends her servants to spy on people, and she's always demanding tribute from everyone.'

'What sort of tribute?' asked Lizzy.

'Sea jewels, rare shells and plants . . . anything, really, which she thinks will make her or her palace more beautiful.' He paused. 'Mother's had to give away her coral necklace, because there wasn't time to find anything else. My great-grandad made it for her, and she really loves it. But Taran always gets whatever she wants.'

'Couldn't people stand up to her?' Lizzy said indignantly. 'There's only one of her, after all. If you got together and said no, what could she do?'

Kes shook his head. 'I told you she's very powerful. I don't know where her power comes from or how she uses it, but she does some really frightening things. When she's angry, she can call up storms. If anyone disobeys her, she punishes them by hurting them, or destroying their homes, or worse. And she doesn't even have to leave her palace to do it – she just uses her power and it happens.'

'What do you mean, "or worse"?' Lizzy was uneasy.

There was a long pause. Then Kes said quietly, 'People disappear.'

'*What?*'

'It's true. There were some cousins of Mother's, who lived in the next bay east of here. They had a beautiful shell, big enough to lie in, made from mother-of-pearl. Taran wanted it, but they refused to give it to her. Next day, some friends went to call on them. The shell had gone, and everything else in their cave had been smashed to pieces. And our cousins had disappeared.' Kes shivered. 'No one's ever found any trace of them.'

Lizzy whistled softly. 'That's terrible!'

'Yes – and it's getting worse. She's taken so much from our people that we've hardly got anything else left to give her. But she still keeps demanding more. I hate her; so do the dolphins and seals and all the friendly sea creatures. And she isn't even the rightful Queen. She's a u . . . u . . .'

'Usurper?' Lizzy had learned about usurping kings in history at school last term.

'That's the word. The old Queen died years ago. She had a daughter, who should have taken her place. But she disappeared, and Taran became Queen instead.' Leaning towards Lizzy, Kes added darkly, 'Mother's always pretended that Taran was *chosen* to be the new Queen, but I don't think that's the way it happened. *I* think there was

something strange about the daughter's
disappearance.'

'You mean, Taran had something to do
with it?'

Kes nodded. 'I've heard rumours. Just
snippets, but enough to make me suspicious.
I heard another story once . . .' He hesitated,
then leaned closer to Lizzy and whispered,
'Some people think she kidnapped the old
Queen's daughter and . . . killed her.'

'But why won't your mother talk about it?
Why doesn't she want you to know the
truth?'

'Because she's trying to protect me. She
thinks I'm too young to understand. Either
that or she's scared I might say the wrong
thing to the wrong person and vanish, like
her cousins did.' He sighed. 'You know what
mothers are like.'

Despite herself Lizzy smiled. But the smile
didn't last. 'So she's frightened, just like
everyone else . . . Have you ever met Taran?'

'No. No one ever sees her. Her palace is far out in the deep sea – no one knows exactly where, but they say the only way to reach it is through some kind of magic gateway. When the merfolk have to pay tribute, she orders them to meet her servants at some place she decides, and they take the gifts to her. Then, if she's not satisfied, the servants come back and say she wants more.'

Lizzy stared out to sea, silent. A false Queen, plots and intrigues and strange powers . . . there was far more to Kes's underwater world than she could ever have imagined.

Then she remembered something else he had told her. 'Kes,' she said, 'you said I was kidnapped when I was a baby. You don't think Taran had anything to do with that, do you?'

He looked thoughtful. 'I don't know. I think it's possible . . . but I've never been able to work out why she'd want to. I mean, we're not important or anything.'

'In that case, why would anyone else have wanted to? It doesn't make sense.' Lizzy stared at the sea again. 'It seems to me that there are a lot of things your mother has never told you. And I'd like to know what they are.'

'I've tried to ask, but she always says she'll tell me when I'm older. Maybe if we *both* talk to her, though . . .'

'Yes. Yes, I think we should. After all . . .' Lizzy hesitated, and then smiled at him, a little sadly. 'She's the only person who can tell me anything about my life under the sea.'

Chapter Eight

Neither Lizzy nor Kes had much to say as they climbed back down the rocks and walked along the tideline. Lizzy stared down at the wavelets foaming around her ankles. She felt an awful sense of anticlimax. She had been so excited about meeting Morvyr, and now she would have to wait at least another day. Even if there was a good reason, it was still an enormous disappointment.

Kes's voice broke into her thoughts, and she looked up. 'Sorry, what did you say?'

'You were fathoms away!' He smiled sympathetically. 'I know what you were thinking, and I'm disappointed too. So I said, why don't we swim for a while?'

'You mean, under the water?'

'Yes.' Kes's smile turned into a grin. 'You could do with the practice, I expect.' Then before she could dodge, he kicked up water with one foot and splashed her.

'Hey!' Lizzy's dismal mood vanished and she splashed him back, using her hands as well for good measure. A water-battle began then, and within seconds they were both soaked and laughing. Finally Lizzy lost her footing and sat down in the shallows. A wave surged in her face and she spluttered, and Kes reached down to haul her to her feet.

'That's better!' he said. 'You look much more cheerful. Come on, we'll slip away while the lifeguards aren't looking.'

Quietly, seen by no one, they moved into deeper water and dived. For the first few moments Lizzy was afraid to try to breathe, but she plucked up her courage and it all happened as naturally as before. She found, too, that her wetsuit made swimming much easier. In fact she could almost imagine that she was a dolphin, sleek and swift in the water.

Kes looked over his shoulder at her and called, 'Let's play follow my leader! Bet you can't do everything I do!'

'Bet I can!' Lizzy called back indignantly.

He grinned. 'We'll see!' And he was off, leading her in a fast and complicated chase. He was very acrobatic, twisting and turning in the water. Lizzy did her best to copy him, and to her own surprise she was able to perform many of the moves he made.

'Not bad!' said Kes when at last the game ended.

Lizzy looked smug. 'Do I win the bet, then?'

'Well . . . nearly. But not quite. There's something I haven't shown you yet, and I bet you *anything* you can't do it. Want to see?'

'**Y**es!' said Lizzy determinedly.

'Right. Then watch this.'

He launched himself away and started to swim round her in a wide circle. Lizzy was puzzled, for he didn't seem to be doing anything special. But then she realized that his shape was beginning to change . . . Amazed, she watched as his legs merged together. Shining scales appeared on them, his feet elongated and became fins . . . and suddenly the transformation was complete, and in place of Kes's human limbs was a fishlike tail. He was no longer an ordinary human – he was a merboy!

'Well?' He swam back to her and gave his tail a flick that made him spin right round. 'What do you think?'

'It's – it's *amazing*! I had no *idea* you could do that!'

Kes grinned. 'It's easy. I'm only half human, remember.' He paused. 'And so are you. If you try, you can learn to do it too.'

'Me?'

'Of course. It's in your nature.'

Lizzy was astounded. Yet when she thought about it, wasn't it obvious? She was Kes's true sister – and that meant she was half mermaid. The thought made her dizzy.

'Come on,' said Kes. 'Why don't you try? Just use your willpower to make it happen.'

He set off, swimming more slowly, and after a moment's hesitation Lizzy followed. *Use your willpower*, Kes had said. She concentrated with all her strength as she tried to make herself change. But though she felt twice that she was almost succeeding, nothing happened and her legs stayed the same.

At last she stopped swimming. 'It's no good,' she said despairingly. 'I just can't.'

'Never mind,' Kes consoled her. 'I didn't really expect you to, not yet. You've never tried before – you didn't even know it was possible until a few minutes ago.'

'But you make it look so easy!'

He laughed, sending a stream of bubbles shimmering upwards. 'Well, I've had eleven years to practise, haven't I? Don't worry, it'll come to you in time. You've just got to be patient.'

'Oh, great. You mean like I've got to be patient about meeting Morvyr?'

Kes's smile faded. 'Yes,' he replied quietly.

Suddenly Lizzy felt mean. 'I'm sorry. I shouldn't have said that. Waiting for her to come back must be awful for you as well.'

He reached out and clasped her hand briefly, but only said, 'We'd better head for the shore. We've come a long way out, what with all those games.'

With a big effort Lizzy made herself cheer up. 'I enjoyed them,' she said. 'And you know what? When I *do* learn to become a mermaid, I'm going to practise and practise and practise my swimming, until I'm even better than you!'

*

Rose smirked across the kitchen table and said, 'Lizzy's got a boyfriend.'

Mum and Dad both looked at Lizzy in surprise, and Lizzy felt her face turning bright red. 'I haven't!' she said defensively.

'No?' Rose's smirk turned into a wicked grin. 'Who's this Kes you're spending all your time at the beach with, then? I saw the two of you, heading up to the old lighthouse.'

'He isn't my boyfriend,' protested Lizzy. 'He's just . . . someone I met.'

Mum saw that Lizzy was getting upset and said, 'Stop teasing her, Rose. If she's making new friends, that's great.' She smiled at Lizzy. 'Who is he, love? A local boy, or someone here on holiday?'

'He's . . . sort of local,' Lizzy mumbled, still red-faced. 'He's the boy who found my locket when I lost it.'

'Well, there you are, Rose! She's got every reason to like him.'

'Anyway, you're a fine one to talk,' Dad

chipped in. 'What with Paul this and Paul that and Paul the other . . . I don't know – you kids!'

'You should invite him round some time,' said Mum to Lizzy. 'Bring him to tea one day.' She looked sidelong at Rose. 'And you can ask Paul too. It's about time Dad and I met him.'

'I'll think about it,' said Rose airily, and as Mum turned away she leered at Lizzy as if to say, 'Wriggle out of that one!'

Lizzy didn't stick her tongue out, as she knew Rose expected her to do, but looked away. She felt desperately uncomfortable, but not because of Rose's teasing. She was thinking about Mum and Dad, and how they would react if they knew the truth about Kes. The Baxters loved her as if she were their own child. How would they feel if they knew that she had found her brother and was soon to meet her *real* mother? Would they be glad? Hurt? Angry? Lizzy didn't know, and she was very confused. Part of her wanted to tell them about her discovery, but deep down she knew she couldn't. Because, if she did, she would have to tell them everything – including the fact that Morvyr was a mermaid, and she herself was only half human. They wouldn't believe it, of course. How could they? They'd think she had invented some crazy fantasy about her own past, and that would upset them. Even if she proved it by showing them that she could breathe underwater, what then? They'd probably be frightened. They might even turn against her. After all, most people would call her a freak. Why should Mum and Dad and Rose be any different? They'd stop loving her. Whatever else happened, Lizzy couldn't bear that.

She realized suddenly that Rose was staring at her, and quickly she forced her face into what she hoped was a normal expression.

'Lizzy?' Rose sounded contrite. 'I didn't

upset you, did I? Sorry – it was only a tease.'

Lizzy managed something like a smile. 'Course you didn't upset me,' she said. 'I'm just . . . a bit tired, that's all.'

'Too much sun, sea and sand,' said Dad.

Both the girls ignored him. 'Tell you what,' Rose went on, 'Paul's going out with his dad on their fishing boat tomorrow. I'm going along to the harbour to see them off. Want to come?'

Lizzy hesitated. She knew this was Rose's way of trying to make up, and she longed to say yes. But what if Morvyr came back, and wanted to see her? For all her worries, nothing was more important than that.

'I . . . er . . . yes, maybe,' she said. 'I'll – think about it.'

Rose shrugged, looking slightly miffed. 'Please yourself,' she said. 'I just thought I'd offer.'

'Thanks.' Lizzy felt guilty. 'I'd like to, I really would if . . . if I can.'

Rose stared curiously at her. But she didn't say anything else.

In bed that night, Lizzy's mind churned with the thoughts that had haunted her earlier, and when she did finally go to sleep she had troubling dreams in which she saw Mum fighting with Taran, the cruel mermaid Queen. Everything was muddle and confusion, and she was thankful when she woke up just after seven o'clock.

For a while she lay in bed, looking at another bright and sunny day outside and trying not to think about anything. She could hear somebody moving around downstairs. Dad, probably; he usually got up before anyone else. She didn't want to go down and talk to him. Right at the moment, she didn't want to talk to anybody.

But it seemed that somebody wanted to talk to her.

At first she didn't know where the sound

was coming from. It was a voice, and she thought it was calling her name. It wasn't Dad, though. Someone outside? She didn't think so and, anyway, it was very distorted. Crazily, the thing that occurred to her was that it sounded like someone using a mobile phone underwater.

Underwater . . .

'Oh!' Lizzy gasped in shock and sat up. The voice was coming from her shell!

She scrambled out of bed and snatched the shell up, holding it to her ear. Sounds of the sea swirled and hissed – then, almost lost among them, she thought she heard her name again.

'Kes?' she cried.

'*Lizzy . . . Lizzy . . .*' Was she really hearing it, or was it her imagination? She couldn't be sure. But a strange feeling was forming in her mind. The beach – she must go to the beach, as soon as she could!

The voice in the shell was fading as the sea

noises surged again. Lizzy's hand shook as she put the shell down, but her eyes were shining. Kes had called to her. She had heard him. And the message she had felt in her bones could only mean one thing. Morvyr must have returned.

She realized that there was a smell of cooking wafting up from the kitchen. Breakfast. But she was far, far too excited to even think of eating. Hastily she threw on the first clothes she could find, and pounded down the stairs.

Dad was at the stove frying bacon and eggs.

'Morning, thunder-feet!' he said cheerfully, and waved his spatula at the frying pan. 'Plenty here for everyone!'

Lizzy skidded to a halt and her face fell. 'Oh . . . no, thanks, Dad. I – I'm not really hungry.'

Dad looked at her with concern. 'You said that yesterday too. I wonder if you're sickening for something?'

Alarmed, Lizzy protested, 'Honestly, I'm fine!'

'Well, it isn't like you not to want breakfast two days running. Maybe I'll have a word with Mum –'

'No!' If Dad and Mum thought there was anything wrong with her, she wouldn't be allowed to go to the beach. There was no choice; she had to play along, and, though her stomach turned over at the thought, Lizzy added hastily, 'Perhaps I will have some, then.'

'That's the girl! Give Mum a call and tell her it's ready, will you?'

'OK. Is she upstairs?'

'Yes, getting dressed. She's going in to Truro this morning, to see about doing some admin work at the hospital.'

'Oh, right.' Mum had worked part-time since the girls were old enough not to need her so much. She'd be pleased if she found a good job so soon after moving here, Lizzy thought. 'What about Rose?' she added.

'I'd leave her, if I were you,' said Dad. 'She seems to have forgotten her early rising craze, and she wouldn't eat this anyway. Then you can sit down and I'll dish it up.'

Somehow Lizzy forced herself to eat an egg, a rasher of bacon and half a tomato. She just hoped she wouldn't be sick later. As she fought her way through it Mum said, 'Are you going to the beach again this morning, or would you rather come to Truro with me and do some shopping after my interview?'

Lizzy's heart thumped. 'Oh . . . the beach, please. It's a bit too hot for town.' She eyed Mum hopefully. 'Is that OK?'

'Yes, fine. But if you're going to swim, stay in sight of the lifeguards, all right?'

'All right.' And Lizzy thought: *Oh, Mum . . . if only you knew!*

Chapter Nine

As soon as she had eaten enough to avoid making Mum and Dad suspicious, Lizzy grabbed her wetsuit and ran all the way to the beach. At this early hour there was hardly anyone around, and as she ran to the sea's edge there was a splashing further out and Kes surfaced.

'You heard me!' he said eagerly as he splashed out of the water to where she stood.

'Yes!' Lizzy's eyes shone. 'It was fantastic – I couldn't really make out what you were saying, but I knew you wanted me to meet you here. Oh, Kes, has Morvyr come back?'

He nodded. 'She got home late last night. And she's sent me to fetch you. She's so excited!'

'Me too.' Lizzy's heart was pounding like a hammer under her ribs. She started to pull her wetsuit on. 'I can hardly believe it – to see her, and to see your home –'

'Well . . .'

Lizzy stopped wrestling with the suit. 'Is something wrong?'

He frowned. 'No, but . . . it's a bit strange, but she doesn't want me to bring you home. She'll meet us at another cave, a bit further down the coast.'

'Why?' Lizzy was baffled.

'I don't know. I asked, of course, but she just said it would be better for all of us.'

It was Lizzy's turn to frown. 'I don't understand. Doesn't she want me to see where you live? After all, it was my home too, once.'

'I don't understand, either. Unless it's got

something to do with what happened to me on my way back yesterday . . .'

'What was that?'

'I kept getting this weird feeling that someone was following me. Watching.' Kes glanced over his shoulder, as if half expecting his mysterious pursuer to appear out of the water. 'I told Mother. She said I shouldn't worry about it, but I wonder if that's what made her decide to meet us somewhere else.'

Lizzy was beginning to feel uneasy. 'You don't know who it was?'

'No. I looked back a few times, but I didn't see anyone. It was just a feeling.'

'What about this morning? Did it happen again when you were on your way here?'

Kes shook his head. 'Arhans and the other dolphins are around, though. Maybe whoever it was – if it was anyone at all – didn't want to get too close to them.'

Lizzy wasn't happy about this. Someone following Kes . . . why? What did they want? And why would they be anxious to keep away from the dolphins? She looked at the sea and said dubiously, 'Are you sure it's safe to go out there now?'

'Oh, yes. Arhans isn't far away. Look, we'd better go before the lifeguards turn up and see us. Are you ready?'

Was she? Lizzy wondered. To meet her real mother at long last . . . was she *really* ready for that?

She pushed her doubts down and swallowed. 'Yes,' she said.

Kes smiled. Then they waded into the water, plunged into the waves and struck out from the shore. Past the surf, they both turned to look back at the beach.

Lizzy's heart was bumping. But she knew, now, what she could do.

Together, they dived under the water.

Again Lizzy's mind reeled with wonder as she followed Kes through the blue-green world just a few metres under the sea. She could still hear the noise of the surf, a kind of rhythmic, thrumming roar, but as they left the land behind it grew fainter. At last it faded away, and there was just the quiet swirl of the current flowing past them. Kes had not changed into a merboy, but all the same he was swimming quickly, urging her to hurry. She concentrated on keeping up with him, and found it surprisingly easy. In the distance she could dimly see other shapes, sleek and fast: a glimmer of silver showed on the side of one, and through the water she heard the dolphins whistling to each other. The knowledge that they were there was very reassuring.

After a while Kes turned and headed towards the surface. Lizzy went after him, and moments later their heads bobbed up into air and sunlight. She was astonished to see how far they had swum. The bay was out of sight, hidden behind a jutting headland. All she could see were the rocky outlines of the coast stretching away towards Land's End. And the sea. For a moment she was frightened – it looked so vast and endless that it made her feel like a tiny helpless speck. But then she remembered what Kes was – and what she was – and the fear went away.

Kes pointed along the coast. 'See those rocks reaching out into the water? That's where we're going. If you look hard, you can make out the cave entrance.'

Lizzy peered, blinking water from her eyes. Just beyond the rocks, a narrow fissure showed in the cliffs.

'Mother will be waiting for us,' Kes added. 'Come on.'

I'm going to meet my real mother. And she's a mermaid . . . Lizzy had said the words to herself over and over again since yesterday, and each time she thought about it, a little lurch of fear made a knot in her stomach. This time, though, there was excitement mingled with it. And it was far too late to turn back.

She gave Kes a nervous smile, and together they dived again.

The water turned green and dim as they neared the cliffs, and the rocks below the surface looked like huge threatening shadows coming to meet them. Above their heads waves were foaming and washing back in great surges, and for a few awful moments Lizzy wondered how they could ever get through to the cave. The dolphins had veered away and disappeared, not wanting to go too close to the treacherous coastline. But Kes took a firm hold of her hand and towed her with him towards a narrow channel. Dark walls rose on either side, seeming to rush past as they swam. Then suddenly there was sand beneath them, and they found their feet and surfaced on a shelving beach inside the cave.

Lizzy could only stare and stare. The cave
had a high arched roof, and the noise of the
sea echoed in it like a singing voice. The
sand they stood on was silvery-white and
very fine. It sloped upwards to a ridge, and
beyond the ridge was a pool of calmer water.
A large rock jutted up from the middle of
the pool.

And on the rock sat a mermaid.

Lizzy's heart gave such an enormous
thump that she felt as if it had turned upside
down under her ribs. The mermaid had hair
of pale white-gold that curled over her
shoulders and cascaded down her back like a
waterfall. It was exactly the same colour as
Lizzy's. Her eyes were grey, like the sea in
winter. But instead of human legs, she had a
long green tail that shimmered with silvery
scales, like the tail of a fish.

Kes said, 'Mother . . . I've brought
Tegenn.'

The mermaid stared at Lizzy, and above

the echoing sea sounds Lizzy heard her gasp. Then she put both hands to her face and said softly, 'Tegenn – is it really you?'

Lizzy began to tremble. Slowly she walked to the edge of the pool and stopped. She and the mermaid gazed at each other. Then Lizzy whispered, 'M-mother . . .?'

'Oh, my little Tegenn!' The mermaid held out her arms, and Lizzy flung herself forward, splashing through the pool to the rock. They hugged each other tightly, both laughing and crying at once, while Kes just stood by with a big happy smile on his face.

At last the crazy excitement died down enough for Morvyr to hold Lizzy at arm's length.

'Let me look at you!' she said. 'Oh, this is such a joyous moment! When Kes said he had found you, I didn't believe it – I *dared* not believe it! But then he told me about your locket. And now that I see you for myself, there can be no doubt. My own lost daughter has come back to me!'

Tears were still streaming down Lizzy's cheeks, and she felt dizzy with an incredible sense of wonder. She could hardly believe that this was happening. It was like a fairy tale, something magical and impossible. And yet somehow it had come true. Like Morvyr, there was no doubt in her mind. She *knew* that she had found her real family at last.

'There are so many things I want to say!' said Morvyr. 'So much to ask and to tell. And the first thing of all . . .' She gazed intently at a spot below Lizzy's neck, and Lizzy realized that she was looking at the mother-of-pearl locket.

'Yes,' said Morvyr softly. 'It *is* the one.' She reached out and took it in her hand. 'Your father made this locket when you were born,' she told Lizzy.

'Th-there's a curl of hair inside,' Lizzy said. 'Everyone always said it must be mine, but I

– I wondered . . .' Her voice tailed off.

'It's mine,' said Morvyr, still smiling. She pressed the catch and the two halves of the shell opened, revealing the pale golden curl. 'Your father's hair was black, like Kes's.'

'I want so much to know more about him,' said Lizzy wistfully. 'What was he like? Was he handsome?'

'Oh, yes.' Morvyr smiled, and her voice caught with emotion. 'He was very handsome – at least, I thought so. Would you like me to tell you our story?'

'Yes! Oh, yes!'

'Please, Mother!' Kes added eagerly. His face clouded. 'You've never really talked about him to me.'

'I know, and I still can't explain everything, not yet. But now that Tegenn has come back to us . . .' She smiled at them both in turn. 'Come and sit here beside me, and I'll tell you what I can.'

Kes and Lizzy exchanged a look. Then Kes

took hold of Lizzy's hand, and they moved to sit on the rock beside their mother.

And outside the cave, concealed by the crowding rocks and almost invisible in the deep greenness of the sea, a pair of cold eyes watched, and a pair of sharp ears listened intently . . .

Chapter Ten

'Years ago,' said Morvyr, 'a man called Jack Carrick was out sailing in the bay when a storm blew up. He tried to run for harbour, but his boat's engine failed and he was carried on to a dangerous reef. The boat was wrecked, and Jack would have drowned, but I was nearby. I saw what was happening, and I rescued him. I brought him to this cave, where he would be safe from the wild sea, and I took care of him.' She smiled sadly, remembering. 'I meant to take him back to land when the storm was over. But, instead, we fell in love.'

'But he was human,' Lizzy said quietly. 'Surely he couldn't live under the sea?'

'That was true,' Morvyr agreed. 'We thought we would have to part, and we were heartbroken. But the Queen of the mermaids – the previous Queen, that is, not the . . . the one who rules now – took pity on us. She had great powers, and she used them kindly and wisely. She made a spell for Jack, so that he could breathe underwater as we can. He couldn't live under the sea all the time, though. Even the Queen wasn't *that* powerful, so every now and then he had to return to land for a while. But it was enough for us. We were married in a merfolk ceremony and, two years later, twins were born to us.'

'Me and Kes?' Lizzy whispered.

'Yes. Jack and I were so happy. But then a dark time came to our world. The Queen died, and the one who followed her was very different.'

'You mean Taran,' said Kes angrily. 'Taran took the Queen's place!'

Morvyr gave him a long look. 'Yes, she did.'

'She killed the real Queen, didn't she, Mother?'

Morvyr looked alarmed. 'You mustn't say such things!'

'But it's true, isn't it? You wouldn't tell me, but I've heard! Arhans says –'

'Arhans shouldn't say such things, either!' Now Morvyr really looked afraid, then with an effort she calmed down. 'Let us just say that she died, and Taran became the new Queen.'

'She's got no right to be Queen! She's a – a –' Kes had forgotten the word again. He looked at Lizzy and she said, 'A usurper.'

'Children.' Morvyr's face was very serious. 'Whatever you think, whatever you hear from anyone, you must never, *ever* say that aloud again. Do you understand me?'

There was a pause. Then Kes replied in a small voice, 'Yes, Mother.'

'Tegenn?'

' . . .Yes,' whispered Lizzy.

'Good. Because, if you do, you could be in danger. I lost Tegenn once. I don't want to lose both of you. Now, listen and I'll tell you the rest of the story.'

Sobered, Kes and Lizzy fell silent, and Morvyr continued. 'A certain person wanted something from your father and me, which we would not give them. So this person waited until Jack had to go away to land for a time, and while he was gone, sh– the person stole our baby daughter in revenge.' She bit her lip. 'I was distraught! I went as close to the shore as I dared and I swam there for days, calling and calling for Jack – I was so desperate that I almost let myself be discovered by humans, which is something a mermaid must never do! At last the dolphins saw him walking on the beach, and they were able to get close enough to tell him what had happened.' She gave a great sigh that echoed around the cave. 'He came back at once. But what could he do? Tegenn was gone. And we didn't know where to begin searching.'

'But Father tried to find her, didn't he?' said Kes. 'That's why he went away.'

'No, he didn't. We believed – we were led to believe – that Tegenn had been taken to a far distant place. Jack promised that he would search the world until he found her, and he left on a ship, thinking he knew where she might be.'

'He didn't find me, though,' whispered Lizzy.

'Yes. I realize now that the kidnapper laid a false trail, to deceive us.' Morvyr's voice caught again. 'Jack never returned, and no one knows what became of him.'

Lizzy felt hot tears pricking her eyes. They trickled down her cheek and she didn't even try to stop them. 'Oh, Mother,' she whispered. 'If only . . .' But she couldn't say any more. What use was 'if only'? It wouldn't bring her father back. They didn't even know whether he was still alive.

Morvyr wiped her eyes and blinked. 'At least I've found you again, Tegenn, and that is such a joy to me. I want to know about your life on land. For instance, I heard Kes call you by a different name. What was it – Lussie? Lishy?'

'Lizzy.' Despite her sadness, Lizzy smiled. 'It's short for Elizabeth.'

'Elizabeth . . . how strange it sounds! What does it mean?'

Lizzy was nonplussed. 'I don't know,' she said. 'I've never thought about it.'

'But all names have meanings. Morvyr means "daughter of the sea". It was my mother's name too, and my grandmother's, and many great-grandmothers' before that. But Jack and I wanted *our* daughter to be different, so we called you Tegenn. It means "little jewel". And Kesson – which is Kes's full name – means "harmonious".'

'"Little jewel" . . . that's lovely!'

'I think Lizzy is lovely too, whatever it means. I would like to call you Lizzy. Is that all right?'

Lizzy hugged her. 'I'd like that too . . . Mother.'

Morvyr's face was radiant as she gazed at Lizzy for a few moments. Then abruptly her face grew very serious.

'Before I hear your story, though, there is one more thing to be done. Please, Lizzy – give me your locket. There's something I *must* be sure of.'

Mystified, Lizzy slipped the silver chain over her head. Morvyr took the locket, opened it, and laid it in the palm of one hand. Then she closed her eyes and, as if remembering something from long ago, moved her fingers over its surface.

There was the faintest *click*. And to Lizzy's

amazement, another tiny compartment
sprang open. She gasped, leaning forward to
look more closely, and saw that inside the
compartment was a beautiful silvery pearl.

'Oh!' Lizzy's eyes shone with delight. 'How
wonderful!'

'It's still here!' Morvyr breathed. Very
gently, she touched the pearl with a fingertip
and whispered, '*Sing* . . .'

A faint, sweet, high note began to ring out
from the locket. To her amazement Lizzy
realized that the sound was coming from the
pearl. Morvyr gazed at it as though in a
trance. She seemed to be listening for
something else, and there was a far-away
look in her eyes. Then her face clouded, and
suddenly she snapped out of her strange
mood and quickly closed the compartment.
The sweet sound vanished, and Lizzy blinked
in bewilderment.

'Mother?'

Morvyr hung the locket back round Lizzy's

neck. 'I had to find out if the pearl was still there,' she said. 'But it isn't safe to let it be seen for more than a few moments. I can't tell you why; all I will say is that it's vitally important that you protect it. You must take it back to land and *never* bring it to the sea world again. Please, Lizzy, promise me you'll do as I ask!'

'I promise, of course,' said Lizzy. 'But why won't you tell me any more?'

'Because it's safer if you don't know,' Morvyr replied. 'Don't tell anyone about it; don't show it to anyone. It must be our secret, until the time is right.' She put a finger to her lips. 'No more questions now. We have happier things to talk about.' Then she smiled, as if nothing strange had happened at all. 'To begin with, I want to hear *everything* about your life on land!'

The eavesdropper had seen and heard enough. Silently, stealthily, he turned and swam away from the coast, heading out to the deep sea. No one saw him go. The dolphins were somewhere else – the rumour he had started about a large shoal of mackerel had seen to that – and the smaller creatures were too afraid of him to do anything other than hide as he passed.

On and on he swam, until he came to a massive solitary rock on the seabed. In the centre of the rock was a deep, wide hollow. The eavesdropper swam to the rock and hovered above it, his cold, cruel eyes staring down. He waited patiently. Then a voice echoed eerily to him, seeming to come from inside the hollow.

'*Who is there?*'

A shiver of pleasure ran the length of the creature's body, and his own harsh voice rang out. 'It is Tullor.'

For a moment nothing happened. Then the invisible speaker said, '*Come.*'

The water in the hollow began to agitate.

It stirred, then swirled, and as the swirling increased the hollow started to glow with a strange crimson light. Tullor moved towards it, closer and closer. As his head touched the rim of the hollow, the crimson light flared to scarlet, spilling outwards until his whole body looked as though it were on fire. Then, with one smooth, swift movement, he vanished into the hole.

Tullor saw the rainbow of light above him and he swam towards it. It grew brighter, and moments later he surfaced in the middle of a huge calm pool in a perfectly circular cave.

The cave had no entrance but was completely enclosed, and the air inside shimmered with light. It was a breathtakingly beautiful place. But Tullor had no interest in beauty. He swam across the pool to where a couch of rock jutted out of the water, and when he reached the couch he bowed his head respectfully and said, 'Your Majesty.'

Taran, self-appointed mermaid Queen, stared haughtily down at him from where she reclined on the rock.

'Well, faithful servant?' she said in a silvery but icy voice. 'What news have you brought?'

Tullor writhed with excitement. 'Your Majesty, the rumour is true – Morvyr's lost daughter has returned!'

'Ah!' Taran clenched her fists eagerly. 'So my suspicions were right!' Her eyes hardened and she stared menacingly at her servant. 'You're sure of this, Tullor? Because if you're mistaken –'

'I'm not mistaken! I saw her with my own eyes only minutes ago. She looks exactly like her mother. There can be no doubt of who she is.'

'I see . . . And does Morvyr know of this?'

'Oh, yes. The boy, Kesson, told her, and brought the girl to her. At this moment Morvyr and both her children are talking together in a cave not far from the place where the human fishermen live.' Tullor shuddered as he said 'fishermen', as though he hated the word. 'But there's more, Your Majesty. The child has one of the missing magical pearls!'

'*What?*' Taran's eyes lit with excitement. 'Are you *sure*?'

'Certain, Majesty. I followed her to the cave and saw the pearl with my own eyes – and I heard it sing!'

'Which pearl is it? Tell me, quickly!'

'The silver, Your Majesty.'

'And the black – does she have the black pearl too?'

'No, madam. Or, if she does, I didn't see it.'

Taran hissed between clenched teeth. 'How could she have come by the silver pearl? It isn't possible!'

'It was inside a locket – a bauble, nothing more – that the girl wears round her neck.'

'What? That locket? I remember it! Morvyr's husband, that wretched human, made one each for his children . . .' Now Taran's eyes blazed with fury. 'They tricked me! *They tricked me!*' She made a wild gesture with one hand, and the water in the pool began to agitate. Waves smacked against the cave walls, and Tullor was tumbled from side to side as the pool churned as though in a violent storm.

'When I think of the time I wasted in the hunt for those pearls!' Taran raged. 'I *always* suspected that Morvyr had them! I had her home searched, every cranny of it. When I didn't find them I took that girl-child in revenge and left her on land – and all along my prize was in the worthless trinket round the baby's neck!' She clenched her fists. 'I was such a *fool*! I should have destroyed them all!'

'But, madam, if you had, you would have lost all hope of finding the pearls!' Tullor cried, gasping as a ferocious wave threw him across the pool again. 'Morvyr was the only one who knew where they were hidden, and no one could have guessed – not even one as powerful as you!'

'That's true . . .' Taran took a deep breath and the water quietened a little as the worst of her fury abated. 'And the human Morvyr married was a cunning creature. He chose the hiding place, I'm sure of that. And I'd take any wager that he hid the black pearl in the other locket! But the boy-child doesn't have it. *So where is that locket now?*'

The pool was much calmer by this time, and Tullor swam back to the foot of the rock where his Queen sat. Gazing up fawningly at her, he said, 'At least we know where the silver pearl is, Your Majesty. That is surely better than nothing?'

Taran stared at him for a moment, and then laughed. 'You are right, faithful servant. And that is thanks to you. Well done, Tullor

– I shall reward you for your cleverness. But first . . .' She tapped a finger on the rock, her expression thoughtful. 'You say the children are with Morvyr now?'

'Yes, Your Majesty.'

'Good. Then from now on, you must forget all your other duties. You will watch the girl, and follow her whenever you can. Make sure no one realizes what you are doing – especially those interfering dolphins!' Her face darkened in a scowl, and the pool started to stir again. But then it settled as the scowl was replaced with a cunning smile. 'I have been patient for eleven years. I can be patient for a little while longer. So I want you to wait carefully for your chance, and when it comes, as it is sure to, you will attack the girl and take that locket with the pearl inside!'

Tullor's face was not made to show pleasure, but Taran could feel his satisfaction as he said, 'Yes, Your Majesty!'

'Don't fail, Tullor,' she told him. 'Don't *dare* fail. Once I have the silver pearl, I will only need one more – the black one – and then I will be all-powerful. I want that pearl, and I will have it. I *must* have it – at any cost!'

Chapter Eleven

There were tears when Lizzy and Morvyr said goodbye, and even Kes was blinking and pretending to have something in his eye. Morvyr gave Lizzy a present of a beautiful ring. It was made from corals of three different colours, pink and blue and green, all twisted together like a tiny rope. It fitted her finger beautifully, and she only wished that she had brought a gift for Morvyr. But they would see each other again soon, and when they did, Lizzy promised herself that she would find something very special to bring her mother from the land.

'Remember,' Morvyr repeated as Lizzy and Kes prepared to leave, 'you must keep the silver pearl safe, and never bring it to the undersea world again.'

'I promise,' said Lizzy solemnly. She longed to find out why Morvyr was so concerned about the pearl, but she knew there was no point in asking. When the time was right, her mother had said, she would be told. Until then, she must be patient.

'Take care of her, Kes, and see her safely to shore!' Morvyr called as the twins slipped into the water. 'Goodbye, Lizzy! Goodbye, my little Tegenn!'

She blew a kiss and Lizzy blew one too. Her vision blurred, then with a final wave she dived after Kes, down into the pool and away towards the entrance of the cave.

They travelled in silence for a while. Kes was swimming slowly, as if he were reluctant to reach the land. Lizzy felt the same. She wanted time to think, and to absorb the wonderful thing that had happened to her today. The thought of going home to her other family made her sad. It would have been so amazing to be able to tell them. Instead, though, she must keep the secret to herself.

Kes looked at her then and spoke for the first time. 'Are you all right?' he asked.

Lizzy nodded. 'Sort of.' There was a pause. 'She – Mother – is so beautiful, isn't she? I'd love to think I might look like her one day.'

Kes smiled. 'You already do. Me, I look like Father, or so Mother says.' His face clouded. 'I wish I could remember him.'

'So do I. And I wish . . .'

'What?'

'Oh . . . it's silly, I know. But one fantastic thing's already happened. I just thought, what if another fantastic thing happened, and he came back.'

'If he's still alive,' said Kes sadly.

'Yes . . . I was wondering about that too. Maybe we'll never know.'

They swam on for a few minutes more, finning their hands and feet and letting the current carry them along. Lizzy was beginning to get used to the deep sea, and now she was more fascinated than afraid. But then in the distance she thought she heard something. It wasn't the sound of the sea; in fact it wasn't really a sound at all but more of a vibration, throbbing through the water.

'Kes . . .' Tensely she reached out and touched his arm. 'Listen. What's that?'

Kes slowed down and stopped. He put his head on one side, frowning. Then his expression became alarmed.

'Quick!' he said. 'It's the engine of a fishing boat – if we don't get out of the way, we could get caught up in the net!'

He grabbed Lizzy's hand and towed her quickly off to the right. Lizzy had no idea which direction the boat was coming from, but Kes seemed to know with an unerring instinct. Sure enough, minutes later she saw the long hull cleaving the sea's surface directly above the spot where they had been. Behind it flowed an undulating shadow, and she glimpsed the outlines of a mesh trailing almost to the seabed.

'Look out for the wake!' Kes warned. 'Dive!'

They dived deeper, but even so the wake churned up by the powerful engine's propeller stirred the water and set them both lurching and rocking. At last the disturbance was over, and the twins regained their balance and stared after the boat as it chugged on its way.

'That was close!' said Kes.

Lizzy was shaken. 'W-would it have killed us?'

'No, not unless we got pulled anywhere near the propeller. But just think what would happen if the fishermen hauled us up from under the sea! We couldn't explain our way out of that, and they'd find out about the merfolk.'

'Would that be so awful?' Lizzy sounded wistful. She was thinking about her family on shore.

Kes shattered her hopes. 'Of course it would! Father told Mother what humans are like. If they knew we existed, they'd stop at nothing to catch us, and then what would happen?'

Lizzy realized what he meant. She could picture it: news headlines flashing around the world, the sea people imprisoned in tanks and aquariums, examined by doctors and scientists . . . Her imagination ran riot as she thought of Morvyr captured and helpless, and she looked aghast at Kes.

He said, 'You see, now, why we have to be so careful.'

Gravely Lizzy nodded. Though the underwater world was a magical and beautiful place, she was beginning to learn that it had its dangers.

They started to swim again, making their

way along the coast towards the beach and the town beyond. They could still hear the fishing boat's engine, but it was faint and far away now, just a vague murmur in the distance.

'When do you think I'll be able to see Mother again?' Lizzy asked.

Kes did not answer. She turned her head to repeat the question, but paused as she saw that he was looking back over his shoulder. There was a frown on his face.

'Kes? What's up?'

Still Kes said nothing for a few more moments. Then: 'I'm not sure. I had this feeling there was something behind us just now . . .'

Abruptly Lizzy remembered what he had said earlier, on the beach. 'Yesterday, when you went home . . . you told me something was following you.'

'Yes.' He sounded strained, and Lizzy felt her heartbeats speeding up.

'Maybe it's one of the dolphins,' she said, trying to boost her confidence.

'It isn't,' said Kes. 'If it was, or any other friend, they'd have called out. Lizzy, we *are* being followed, I'm sure of it.'

Fearfully Lizzy peered through the water. She couldn't see very far before the currents blurred everything – but for a moment she thought she glimpsed a long dark shape gliding behind them.

Kes said quietly, 'Swim faster. Let's see what happens.'

Trying not to let dread get the better of her, Lizzy kicked powerfully with her feet. Their pace increased until she could feel the pressure of water rushing past her face.

Kes glanced back again and said, 'It's still there. It's keeping up.'

'Wh-what do you think it is?'

'I don't know.'

'You're not . . . scared, are you?'

'Course not.' But he didn't sound too sure.

They were moving very quickly now. But the follower was quicker. Lizzy dared to glance back, and what she saw filled her with alarm. The shape looked bigger – it was gaining on them.

'It's faster than we are!' she cried. 'It's chasing us!'

There could be no doubt now; whatever lurked behind them in the sea was rapidly coming closer. Another minute, maybe less, and it would catch up with them. Suddenly, instinctively, they both knew that it was an enemy.

'Swim, Lizzy, swim!' Kes yelled. 'Make yourself become a mermaid! You can do it! You can! You've *got* to!'

Even as he called out, his own shape was changing. Lizzy saw his silvery-green tail swish, powering him through the water, and frantically she tried to will herself to change too. *I am a mermaid, I am, I am, I AM!* But she was close to panic now, and couldn't focus her mind. All she could think about was the unknown terror pursuing them. She couldn't outswim it, it was going to catch her, and then –

'LIZZY, LOOK OUT!!' Kes screamed.

Suddenly there was a noise like thunder in the sea, and to her horror Lizzy saw the barrel-like underside of another fishing boat coming straight towards them. White water churned behind it – and something else. A net, skimming through the sea and scooping up anything too big to wriggle through its mesh –

'*Turn, Lizzy, turn!*' Kes was yelling. '*Get away from it!*' He twisted in the water, swift as a fish as he darted out of the net's path. But Lizzy had no tail, and though she kicked with all her strength, she knew that it wasn't going to be enough. The light dimmed as the boat sailed overhead, and the throb of its engine seemed to fill the whole world. Kes had vanished and she didn't know where he was – all she could see was the net, like a shimmering wall, gliding relentlessly towards her.

When the impact came, it was far harder than she expected. Lizzy gasped, sending a torrent of bubbles streaming from her mouth, and next moment she was tumbling over and over as the net swept her along. Her arms and legs tangled in the mesh; she was trapped, caught, powerless –

'Help!' Lizzy cried. 'Oh, someone, please, *help me*!'

Chapter Twelve

'Lizzy! Lizzy!'

Kes shouted his sister's name, but his voice was lost amid the racket of the fishing boat's engine. He could see her struggling in the folds of the net, and as the boat churned on he swam frenziedly after it. But even as he surged towards the net he knew there was nothing he could do. He wasn't strong enough to free Lizzy, and if he went too close, he would be caught as well. He needed more strength – he needed help, as he had never needed it before!

With the engine noise pounding in his ears,

he didn't hear the shrill, high whistling that cut through the water. But when five sleek, grey shapes came streaking towards him, and he saw the flash of silver on the back of their leader, his despair turned to a surge of joy.

'Arhans!' Kes waved frantically towards the net. 'Help Lizzy! Help her!'

In her tangling prison Lizzy cried out in relief as the dolphins attacked the net. Their powerful bodies barged against it and their tail-flukes flipped the folds aside, clearing a path through to her. Sharp teeth tore at the mesh; Lizzy's arms came free and she reached out to grasp hold of Arhans's dorsal fin. More tearing; she kicked, hard, and with a rush she broke free of the net as Arhans towed her away and clear of the danger.

'Lizzy!' Kes swam to her and wriggled in among the group. In the confusion his tail made him look like a small dolphin himself. Lizzy was gasping, still clinging to Arhans as she fought to get over the shock and fright.

The fishing boat chugged on, the men on board unaware of what had just happened, and as the noise of the engine gradually faded, Arhans whistled urgently. Kes listened, and then turned worriedly to Lizzy.

'We're not out of danger yet! The creature that was following us is still around – Arhans says we've got to get away from it as quickly as we can!'

Lizzy looked at him in dismay. Her struggles in the net had taken what was left of her energy. Another fast swim would be too much for her – she just couldn't do it. But then Arhans whistled again, and Kes's eyes lit up.

'Yes! Lizzy, get on to her back – she'll carry you!'

Arhans nudged Lizzy's hands encouragingly and, wide-eyed, Lizzy let Kes guide her on to the dolphin's back. Then to her surprise he changed back to an ordinary boy, and settled astride one of the other dolphins.

'I'm not going to miss out on a chance like this,' he said, grinning. 'Ready? Then hold tight!'

And they were off.

It was an exhilarating and incredible ride – almost as incredible to Lizzy as her discovery that she could live underwater. The dolphins were faster than racehorses, faster than birds. *This must be what flying's like!* Lizzy thought as they swooped and dived through the sea. Rocks and weeds flashed by, shoals of fish darted out of their path, colours streamed past as they raced through the ever-changing world under the waves. Every now and then the dolphins streaked up to the surface to breathe, lifting Lizzy and Kes momentarily out of the water in a whirl of foam. Lizzy gripped tightly with hands and knees, her face alight and her hair flowing behind her. She felt as wild and free as Arhans and her friends – and all thoughts of enemies or danger were gone, for no creature could hope to match them in this wonderful, helter-skelter race.

She wished that the ride would never have to end, but at last the dolphins broke surface one last time and they burst out into sun and air. Clinging tightly, Lizzy cried out with delight as Arhans leaped high out of the water, then curved gracefully over to plunge down again in a fountain of spray. The coast was ahead of them. Lizzy could see the long golden ribbon of the beach with the surf breaking on it, dazzling white in the sun. The beach was crowded, and suddenly she remembered the lifeguards. They would be watching the sea, and they had binoculars. How could she and Kes get to shore without being noticed?

'Kes!' she shouted breathlessly. 'What about the lifeguards? They'll see us!'

Kes laughed. 'Leave that to Arhans! Just be ready to jump off when I say, and she'll do the rest!'

The dolphins were leaping on through the water and the ride was now like a switchback. Closer and closer to land – then Kes called, '*Now!*'

They let go of their dolphins' fins and dived into the sea.

'Come on,' said Kes as they surfaced again and bobbed on the swell. 'Follow me.'

He swam towards the jutting headland where the lighthouse stood. The dolphins were nowhere to be seen. Lizzy was amazed, wondering how they could have vanished so quickly, and as she followed Kes towards the rocks she said, 'Where have they gone?'

He grinned mischievously. 'Look at the beach.' Mystified, she turned round. 'Now,' said Kes, 'watch this.'

Putting two fingers to his lips, he made a sound that was astonishingly like the whistle of a dolphin. Moments later, just off the far end of the beach, Arhans and her four friends leaped high out of the sea in perfect unison. There were shouts of delight as people saw them, and everyone – including the lifeguards – ran to the water's edge to watch. The dolphins leaped again, twisting in mid-air, putting on an acrobatic display.

'That'll keep everybody busy!' said Kes. 'Come on – let's go ashore.'

They swam to the beach and waded, dripping, out of the water. No one was looking in their direction; every single person was engrossed in watching the leaping, dancing dolphins.

For a few moments Lizzy gazed at Arhans and her friends, then very suddenly her legs gave way under her and she sat down on the sand.

'Wow . . .' she said.

Kes knew that she didn't just mean the dolphins' show. He crouched down beside her, then reached out and ruffled her wet hair.

'How are you feeling?' he asked.

Lizzy thought about that. 'Fine – I think.

A bit shaky, maybe. I mean, so much has
happened since this morning . . .' Suddenly
she was afraid she might cry. Fiercely she bit
the impulse back and managed a watery
smile. There were so many questions going
round in her head. She was overjoyed to
have discovered her real mother and brother,
but the knowledge that she was half human
and half mermaid was still almost impossible
to believe. And there were so many
mysteries. The silver pearl hidden in her
locket – she had seen the light shining from
it and heard it sing. What did that *mean*?
Why was it so important to Morvyr – and
why was she afraid? Who was the
mysterious enemy that had followed them in
the sea? What had become of her father?

She tried to say all these things to Kes, but
she could hardly get the words out. Kes
understood, though.

'I feel the same as you,' he told her. 'And I
don't know why Mother won't explain

everything.' He paused. 'Perhaps she's trying to protect us.'

'Perhaps. But I wish we knew what from.'

'Me too.' Kes looked along the beach. The dolphins had gone, and the people who had been watching them were slowly making their way back to their rugs and picnics. 'I'll ask Arhans. Maybe she knows. And if she doesn't . . . well, Mother might change her mind and tell us.'

'And if *she* doesn't?' said Lizzy.

'Then perhaps we can solve the mystery for ourselves. We've found each other now, and we can spend time together and be friends. We've got a lot of catching up to do.'

Lizzy walked home very slowly. She had so much to think about, and was almost afraid to return to the sheer everydayness of the house and her family. Her *other* family. It was so confusing. How could she go back to being just ordinary Lizzy Baxter, when she was also Tegenn, daughter of a mermaid? If only she could tell Mum, Dad and Rose. But that was impossible.

She felt bewildered and a little bit scared as she went in at the back door. Mum was in the kitchen, taking some washing out of the machine.

'Hello, love,' she said, smiling. 'Did you have fun at the beach?'

Lizzy made herself smile back. 'Yes, Mum. It was lovely.'

'Good. You look as if you've been in the sea all day!'

'Er . . . yes, I suppose I have.'

The inner door banged open and Rose came breezing in. 'Hi, Lizzy!' She sounded very cheerful. 'Mum, there's a disco in town tonight. Is it OK if I go with Paul?'

'Yes, I expect so. Provided we know what time you're getting back.' Mum gathered up the washing and went outside, and Rose grinned at Lizzy. 'How's your boyfriend?'

'He's not –'

But Rose had spotted something, and pounced on Lizzy's hand. 'What's this, then? Getting engaged, are you?'

Lizzy had meant to take off the ring Morvyr had given her before she got home, but with so much else on her mind she had completely forgotten. She tried to pull her hand away, but Rose held on, turning it over as she studied the corals. 'That's gorgeous! Seriously, where did you get it? One of the local shops? I'd love one!'

She smiled, and suddenly Lizzy's uncertainty faded away. There was no harm in Rose's teasing. They were the best of friends, always had been. In all the ways that mattered, they were sisters.

She met Rose's eager gaze very steadily and said, 'It was a present, Rose. A very special present.'

Rose looked back at her. She obviously

wanted to ask more questions . . . but something stopped her. Instead she patted Lizzy's hand and let it go.

'Lucky you,' she said. 'Don't worry – I won't say a word to anyone.' And she followed Mum into the garden.

Lizzy went up to her bedroom. The shell Kes had given her was still on the shelf; she picked it up and took it to the window seat that looked out to the sea. The sun was bright and warm on her face as she put the shell to her ear. For a few moments all she could hear was a soft rushing, like waves on a distant beach. But then, gradually, it began to change. As though her mind was slowly attuning, Lizzy heard the mysterious and magical sounds of the undersea world. *Her* world. She smiled. There were voices in the shell, and among them were the voices of her brother, Kes, and her friends, the dolphins. It was almost as if they were saying to her: 'Welcome home.'

Epilogue

When one of the water-mirrors on the cave wall began to glow with crimson light, Taran leaned eagerly towards it. 'Who is there?' she said.

'It is Tullor.' Reflections stirred in the mirror and she saw her servant's face. He looked – and sounded – angry.

'Come!' she commanded, and made a gesture with one hand. The face vanished, then the water of the pool began to swirl, and moments later Tullor surfaced through the magical gateway.

'Well?' said Taran. 'Do you have news?'

'Yes, Your Majesty,' said Tullor harshly. 'But it is not good news. I almost captured the girl-child and took the pearl from her – but I was thwarted by the dolphins! They appeared suddenly, they freed the girl and they carried her and her brother away on their backs to shore.' He writhed furiously. 'I did my best, Your Majesty, but they were too many and too fast for me.'

Taran frowned. She, too, was angry, and she rounded on him. 'You are a fool!' she said savagely. Her hand came up. Tullor cringed – then suddenly Taran changed her mind and lowered her hand again. 'Ah, never mind. There will be other chances.' Her fingernails drummed on the rock. 'So . . . it seems that Arhans and her meddling friends are guarding the wretched girl and her treasure. No doubt Morvyr has persuaded them, and that will make our task harder. But I won't be defeated!'

'What can we do, madam?'

'Oh, there are many ways to catch a fish, Tullor. And I have an idea. A much more subtle idea than mere attack. We shall wait a while – long enough for Morvyr to relax her vigilance a little – and then you, with more of my strongest and fiercest servants, will pay her a visit and arrest her. She will be my hostage – and the price of her freedom will be the silver pearl.'

Tullor made a strange, ugly sound at the back of his throat, almost like a discordant purr. 'My Queen, you are as wily as ever!'

She laughed, pleased by the compliment. 'It will amuse me to have Morvyr as my prisoner for a while,' she gloated.

'Oh, yes, Your Majesty!' Tullor made another ugly sound that was his own version of laughter. 'You could send her to your far stronghold, the place of darkness. She would find that very unpleasant. And she would be company for your *other* prisoner.'

Taran smiled cruelly. 'That would be

fitting. But I do not want anyone to know about that other prisoner. It suits me better if they all think *she* is dead. No, I shall keep Morvyr here until the girl-child gives me the silver pearl.' Her eyes narrowed and a cold, calculating smile spread across her lovely face. 'And don't worry, Tullor – I don't think we shall have long to wait!'